* * *

"Smart And Beautiful."

Laura felt her feathers rise. Did everyone have to mention her face in the first ten seconds of conversation? "Want a cookie?"

"No, thank you."

"Don't tell me you don't like chocolate-chip cookies?"

"No."

"Aah, you won't come into the light to get one."

Silence.

"What else do you deny yourself because you choose to stay in the dark, Mr. Blackthorne?" With her last word, she tossed a cookie in his direction. His hand shot into the light, snatching it from the air.

"And what will you deny your daughter?"

He scoffed. "You know nothing of me, beauty queen."

"You're right, I don't. Just as you know nothing of me...beast."

Dear Reader,

Welcome to the world of Silhouette Desire, where you can indulge yourself every month with romances that can only be described as passionate, powerful and provocative!

Popular author Cait London offers you *Gabriel's Gift,* this April's MAN OF THE MONTH. We're sure you'll love this tale of lovers once separated who reunite eighteen years later and must overcome the past before they can begin their future together.

The riveting Desire miniseries TEXAS CATTLEMAN'S CLUB: LONE STAR JEWELS continues with *Her Ardent Sheikh* by Kristi Gold, in which a dashing sheikh must protect a free-spirited American woman from danger.

In *Wife with Amnesia* by Metsy Hingle, the estranged husband of an amnesiac woman seeks to win back her love…and to save her from a mysterious assailant. Watch for Metsy Hingle's debut MIRA title, *The Wager,* in August 2001. Barbara McCauley's hero "wins" a woman in a poker game in *Reese's Wild Wager,* another tantalizing addition to her SECRETS! miniseries. Enjoy a contemporary "beauty and the beast" story with Amy J. Fetzer's *Taming the Beast.* And Ryanne Corey brings you a runaway heiress who takes a walk on the wild side with the bodyguard who's fallen head over heels for her in *The Heiress & the Bodyguard.*

Be sure to treat yourself this month, and read all six of these exhilarating Desire novels!

Enjoy!

Joan Marlow Golan

Joan Marlow Golan
Senior Editor, Silhouette Desire

Please address questions and book requests to:
Silhouette Reader Service
U.S.: 3010 Walden Ave., P.O. Box 1325, Buffalo, NY 14269
Canadian: P.O. Box 609, Fort Erie, Ont. L2A 5X3

Taming the Beast
AMY J. FETZER

Published by Silhouette Books
America's Publisher of Contemporary Romance

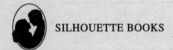 SILHOUETTE BOOKS

ISBN 0-373-76361-1

TAMING THE BEAST

Copyright © 2001 by Amy J. Fetzer

AMY J. FETZER

was born in New England and raised all over the world. She uses her own experiences in creating the characters and settings for her novels. Married more than twenty years to a United States Marine and the mother of two sons, Amy covets the moments when she can curl up with a cup of cappuccino and a good book.

Dedicated with love to my oldest son, Nickolas

For "squishy" hugs and "mambo with me" moments.
For never being afraid to kiss me in front of your friends.
For making me laugh, *really* listening when I lectured,
and wanting this one for yourself. You're a real
gentleman, Nick, and you've made me very proud.

You're destined to be a true hero.

I love you.

One

Laura Cambridge looked up at the gray stone castle and wondered what she'd find inside. Prince Charming or the dragon?

The dragon most likely, she thought, if there was any truth to the gossip the townsfolk were more than willing to share during the ferry ride to this beautiful little island. Did Richard Blackthorne know how much he was feared, she wondered, her gaze moving over the ominous stones and the arched windows as the cab proceeded up the steep driveway. Lord, the structure even had turrets and crenellations. And a tower.

Laura saw only the loneliness of it all.

"Ma'am," the driver said when he stopped before the huge house. "You sure you're supposed to be *here?*"

Why did everyone in this little island village ask that, as if she were walking to her execution? Blackthorne was just a man, for pity's sake. "Oh, yes, I'm sure, Mr. Pinkney," she said, without looking at the middle-aged cabdriver.

"Mr. Blackthorne ain't exactly the most congenial sort, you know."

"With everyone acting as if he'd take a bite out of them, it's a wonder, don't you think?" She looked at him now, arching a brow.

He reddened a bit, then looked back at the house. "Idea had to come from somewheres," he drawled, then rolled out of the driver's seat to get her bags.

Laura left the car, walking with him up the steep front steps.

Summoned like a serf to the king, she had been hired to help Richard Blackthorne's four-year-old daughter adjust to living here. To living with a recluse, a man locked in a castle and shielded from any human contact. Oh, this was going to take some work, she thought, for she knew from the gossip that no one had set foot inside this house, except delivery personnel, in four years. Laura felt instant pity for the little girl, who'd just lost her mother and had been kept from her father. Laura was here early to grow accustomed to the surroundings before the child arrived.

Mr. Pinkney set her bags down. She turned to pay the man and found him jotting something down on a slip of paper. As she handed him the fare, he handed her the paper.

"This here's my number. If you're needin' a ride outta here or anything, you just give me a holler."

She was touched, but it wasn't necessary. "He's not a monster, Mr. Pinkney."

"Yes, ma'am, he is. He snaps and growls at anyone who steps on his land and he made mincemeat out of the delivery boy, and he was just bringing in groceries. I hate to think of what he'd do to you." When Laura gave him a determined look, Mr. Pinkney looked up at the castle. Sighing, he went on. "This here house was built by a man years ago for his bride. She wanted to live like a princess, and he designed and built this house for her. Had every stone brought over from the mainland, some all the way from England and Ireland, to hear tell it. She died before it was finished, or before the fella had a chance to marry her."

How sad, she thought, then tipped her head. "You act as if it's cursed or haunted or something."

Mr. Pinkney said nothing, staring at the wide-arched double slabs of wood as if they were the mouth of a cave. Haunted my fanny, she thought, and lifted the cool brass knocker, smiling to herself. It was the head of a dragon. *Well, Mr. Blackthorne, if you wanted to keep the public away, you're certainly doing a good job at it.* She let the knocker fall.

Instantly a voice came over the intercom to the right of the doors. "Come in."

The voice was deep, sandy-rough, the growling sound of it sending shimmers of apprehension over her skin.

"See what I mean?" Pinkney said.

"Hogwash," she replied firmly, and opened the door, stepping inside. A small lamp on a beautifully carved side table cast the foyer in shadows. She set her purse and briefcase down, then turned to find Mr. Pinkney pushing her bags inside and making a hasty retreat back to the front steps. But that didn't stop him from getting an eyeful of the house, she thought. She flipped on the light switch, and the foyer was flooded with light. He flinched and back-stepped farther.

"You call, you hear," he said, his southern drawl more pronounced.

His attitude, much like that of the folks she encountered in town—the shock, the warnings, and mostly the horrid way people felt they could openly ridicule a man they'd never met—made her feel unaccountably protective of Mr. Blackthorne.

"That won't be necessary," she said, and closed the door. Sighing hard, Laura turned, her heart skipping to her throat as the light went off and a figure loomed at the top of the polished curving stairs.

"Mr. Blackthorne?"

"Obviously." His gravelly voice rumbled down the staircase to her.

"Hello, I'm—"

"Laura Cambridge, I know," he cut in. "Barely thirty, single, USC graduate, raised in Charleston, formerly Miss South Carolina, Miss Jasper County, Miss Shrimp Festival." There was a smirk in his tone then, she swore. "Have I left anything out?"

Well, wasn't he the superior being, she thought, staring up at where he stood on the landing, shrouded in shadows. "You forgot former State Department attaché, embassy schoolteacher, and a linguist, fluent in Italian, Farsi and Gaelic."

"But can you cook?" he said in flawless Gaelic.

"I wouldn't be here if I couldn't." She folded her arms over her waist and regarded the hulking shadow of a man, the foyer light offering only a look at the razor-sharp creases of his dark trousers breaking over his shoes. His hand rested on the banister, a heavy gold signet ring caught the light. Lord, he had big hands, she thought, then said, "So, do I have a Web site or something that I'm not aware of?'' And just how much did he know about her, she wondered.

''Telecommunications is an amazing resource.''

''Yeah, well, spare me from listing my bra size or the time I lost my pom-poms under the bleachers with Grady Benson,'' she said.

''Is that all you lost?'' The words came out in a low growl that tingled up her spine.

It irritated her further. ''Search the Net and find out,'' she snapped, not liking at all that he knew so much about her and she didn't know diddly about him. She hadn't had the chance to find out anything much, except that he'd been reclusive since a disfiguring accident, divorced, and that he would, in a couple of days, take in a daughter he had never met. Curiouser and curiouser, she thought as she took hold of her bags. She faced him. ''Where do I stay?''

''The second floor.''

She walked to the staircase.

''Leave the bags. Follow me,'' he said.

Laura set the suitcases down, yet kept her briefcase and purse with her as she trailed him. He walked several steps ahead of her, as if he could anticipate her stride, always keeping himself in the dark. His walk was smooth, almost elegant, and what little light there was came not from the ceiling but glimmered along the floorboards. All she could see was the outline of his shoulders in the pristine white shirt, broad and straight. Impenetrable. He stopped at a door and quickly shoved it open.

''Here,'' he said, and kept walking.

She stopped outside the room. ''And your daughter's room?''

He hesitated for the briefest instant. ''Across the

hall." He was halfway up a second set of stairs. "I'll have your bags brought up."

"I thought you lived alone?"

"I do. There is a groundskeeper who lives in the cottage behind the house and a maid who comes on Mondays."

"Don't you think we should discuss your daughter's arrival?" she shouted, since he hadn't stopped walking.

"She will be here in two days. Meet her at the ferry." He took each stair with such slow deliberation, Laura wondered if he was in pain.

"You won't come with me?"

"That's why I hired you, Miss Cambridge."

"But you can't mean to just pass your daughter off—"

A door closed with a resounding thump, somewhere up at the top of the stairs. Somewhere in his dark retreat.

"Well, that was productive," she said, and stepped closer to the staircase, looking up. All she could see beyond the upper landing was a hallway and a large polished wood door with a brass latch handle. How could he be so indifferent? Kelly was a baby, for pity's sake, barely four. And was he so badly disfigured that he wouldn't come into the light, or was he just vain? Regardless, it was Kelly she was concerned about, and straightening her shoulders, she climbed the staircase and knocked, hard.

"I believe we need to have a discussion, Mr. Blackthorne. Now."

No answer.

"I can be very persistent if I've a mind to, you know."

"Go away, Miss Cambridge. I will summon you when and *if* you are needed."

"Of course, *your lordship,* how stupid of me to think you actually cared about your only daughter," she said bitterly, and turned on her heels. Pigheaded man, ill-mannered, rude. Her daddy would have knocked him in the teeth for talking to a woman like that.

Laura strode into her room and skidded to a stop, instantly losing her breath. Oh, but the dragon man had good taste. The decor was lavish, the carpet, drapes and even the mats on the paintings blended with the plush furnishings in a scheme that was as sensual as it was relaxing. A large four-poster bed loomed in a corner, draped and covered in thick down comforters, mounds of pillows, and like the room, cast in burgundy, dove-gray and white. There was a Queen Anne-style desk with a computer system resting against the wall near the doors, a cluster of delicate feminine furniture positioned a yard or two before the fireplace, and a padded bench built into a set of three dormer windows, the needlepoint pillows making it look so inviting. To the left was a huge walk-in closet that she could never begin to fill, but darned if she wouldn't like to try, and a bathroom, modern, thank the Lord, with the biggest tub she'd ever seen. Tossing her briefcase and purse on the bed, she crossed the hall and entered Kelly's room.

She stopped short. My word. Apparently money was not a problem for Richard Blackthorne. The room was almost dreamlike, a pink-and-mint-green fantasy in fairy tales with a Victorian dollhouse, new toys galore, and a bed situated at an angle in the corner, its half canopy with sheer curtains draping back to the elaborately carved headboard and caught in rich satin bows. The story of the Princess and the Pea instantly came to mind, for the little girl would have to use that step stool to climb into the high bed. He'd thought of everything, she decided, inspecting the closet and drawers and finding them stocked with clothes in three sizes. He really didn't know anything about his daughter, she realized, and went back to her room, opened her briefcase and slipped out the file Katherine Davenport, owner of Wife, Incorporated, had given her only two days ago.

The face of a little dark-haired girl peered back at her from the photograph, her smile infectiously sweet, her eyes as blue as a Carolina summer sky. Tossing the photo aside with a sigh, she moved to the window bench, brushing back the curtain as she sat down. She could see the mainland and the other islands that were scattered along this portion of the southern South Carolina coast. The October wind whipped over the beach and blew the tall, willowy sea oats like palm fronds in the tropics. Waves rushed the shore, darkening the sand, the sky a dull gray and heavy with moisture. Gloomy. The best time to curl up with a book and dream. And what did a little girl dream about, she wondered, especially one who'd lost her mother and was about to come to an isolated island and meet the father she didn't know she had.

She dreamed of a prince to keep her safe, Laura thought.

Not a dragon who breathed fire when anyone dared step into his cave.

His back braced against the door, Richard closed his eyes, her image locked in his mind and refusing to leave. She was the most beautiful creature he'd ever seen. The kind of woman who made heads turn, men stumble over themselves and women envy them. And just to look into her jade-green eyes made him feel every scar with fresh stinging pain. It was like dangling candy before a starving man. Offer him the sweet, yet deny him a taste.

He could bearly tolerate her being here, in his home, in his sanctuary. Just knowing she was near would drive him mad, he thought, and he wanted to strangle Katherine Davenport for sending him such an exquisite female. Didn't Kat realize he hadn't been near a woman since the accident? And until this morning he didn't even have a name to reference, only Katherine's word that she'd found someone who was qualified. He hadn't been able to do a deep probe of her past, and although he'd found only a portion of it, there were no photographs of her, not that he'd needed them once he'd learned about her pageant wins. Still, it was as if she didn't want that pretty face to be seen. *He* had good reason for that, but what was hers?

She was still gorgeous at thirty.

Damn. He'd been specific on his requirements for a nanny—matronly, strong and healthy enough to chase after a four-year-old and one who understood that the responsibility of Kelly would be hers. He couldn't let Kelly see him. Not ever. The child would run from him, and Richard knew he couldn't take that. Not again. People shunned him because of his disfigurement. He wasn't about to scare a child.

Kelly. Richard clenched his fists. A child he hadn't known existed until a couple of weeks ago when his wife was killed. It seems he was only good enough to care for his own child when there was no other option.

He cursed Andrea again and again for not telling him she was carrying his child when she left him. God, how he'd needed to know that four years ago, for something to hold on to in his world of surgeries and recovery and the hard reality that nothing could be done to change his torn body.

Pushing away from the door, Richard picked up the phone, punching a number with a vengeance.

"Wife Incorporated. Katherine Davenport speaking."

"Dammit, Kat, she's beautiful." Breathtaking, exotic, he added silently, remembering every curve of her body in the tailored white suit.

"So, you came out of your lair long enough to actually look?"

"Why did you do this?"

Her sigh was audible. "Laura is one of the kindest women I know. And I didn't do it for you, sugah. I did it for Kelly. Laura loves children, and she's worked with kids before. She has all the qualifications you wanted. She's educated, but not so much that she can't talk to a child. Besides, she's fun and creative. Give her a chance."

"I don't have a choice. Kelly arrives in two days."

"It will work out, Richard."

"Find someone else, immediately. I don't want her here."

There was a pause on the line, and when Katherine spoke her voice was crisp and cool. "Andrea should have told you about Kelly, I will agree with that, and if I hadn't sworn an oath not to tell you, I would have. But when she said she'd left you because you'd turned cold and mean, I couldn't believe it. I see now that she was right."

Richard felt as if she'd slapped him. "Andrea left because she couldn't handle the repercussions of the accident. She wanted me to look the same and act the same. It was never going to happen. And it never is." He drew in a breath. "Find someone else." He hung up the phone without saying goodbye, his fingers tightening on the receiver before he released it and moved behind his desk.

He dropped in the leather chair and swung it around to face the window. The sun struggled to push through the clouds and sparkle on the river, and Richard forced the memories back, banishing the accident, the tearing pain, and Andrea's reaction when they'd taken off the bandages. Horror. Repugnance. He'd always felt Andrea would be there, beside him, and he was stunned when she left. He should have seen it coming when she wouldn't share his bed, wouldn't touch him after the accident. He saw her revulsion every time he reached for her. The night before the crash was the last time he'd felt the tender wash of pleasure with a woman.

And now a woman voted most beautiful in the state was living in his house. It didn't matter that it was ten years ago, she could still stop traffic.

The knock was so soft he almost didn't hear it.

"Mr. Blackthorne."

Something slammed through him at the sound of her voice, so southern and delicate. He almost hated her for it. "I said I would summon—"

"Gee, last I recall, my job description required that I take care of your daughter, not you. So you can summon and demand all you like, *my lord*—"

"I pay your salary."

"Big deal."

He arched a brow and twisted around to glare at the door.

"And didn't your mother teach you it was rude to interrupt a lady?"

"Didn't you learn diplomacy in the State Department?"

"Yes, but this is not foreign soil, and you can't claim diplomatic immunity."

Fighting a smile, Richard leaned his head back into the leather chair. "What do you want?"

"Aah, the negotiation stage," she said with relish. "Now, unless that rather bland pile of groceries in the fridge and freezer is your idea of a balanced diet, I think I need to do the menu planning."

"Fine. Order whatever you like."

Laura sighed and let her head loll forward. What a difficult man. She jiggled the tray, letting the beautiful china clink. "Hear that? It's dishes, with *food* on them," she said enticingly.

"Leave it at the door."

She blinked. "Excuse me?"

"Surely you heard, Miss Cambridge, the door is not that thick."

"Apparently your head is," she muttered.

"Set it on the floor and leave."

Laura set it down, and when she straightened, she glared at the wood, determined to get him out of that cave. "We are going to have a real hard time at this, Mr. Blackthorne."

"Only if you break the rules."

"And they are?"

"I will e-mail them to you on your computer."

"My, how positively sterile."

''It's the only way,'' he said softly when he heard her footsteps on the staircase.

Richard rubbed his forehead, his fingertips grazing the scars, and he cursed, thrust out of his chair and began pacing. Grinding his teeth, he wondered how he was going to survive with that gorgeous *mouthy* fantasy strutting around his house.

Laura did the dishes with a vengeance. She shouldn't be so upset. What was it to her if he stayed in his sanctuary and brooded? But Kelly would come into this. She couldn't let a child who was expecting to see her daddy, feel the instant exclusion Richard Blackthorne dealt with a few choice words. He wanted no contact whatsoever.

We will just see about that, she thought, throwing a load of laundry in the washer and deciding to investigate the house. Her sneakers squeaked as she walked down the wide hallways, decorated with medieval furnishings. A suit of armor, shields and at least three swords. This guy went all out, she thought, sparing only a brief glance in the other rooms, noticing a painting, an antique settee and a vase so delicate she thought looking at it too hard would crush it.

She walked into the living room. Or was it the parlor or study? She'd passed a couple of locked rooms and figured Mr. Blackthorne didn't want anyone in there and wondered idly if one of them was the dungeon. Well, there were enough nooks and crannies that it would take days to discover them all. And she already surmised that the top floor was off-limits. She threw open the patio doors, and the warm, moist wind hit her face like a gentle, frothy caress. She breathed deeply, tasting salt in the air, and closing the doors behind her, she took off down the beach. It was a pleasure she couldn't resist. Her feet dug into the sand as she pushed her muscles, then she threw her arms out and laughed. *Oh, this isn't so bad,* she thought, folding over to catch her breath. Of course, she should be in better shape. Straightening, she looked back at the house, the castle on the hill. A little hitch caught in her chest. It was the place of dreams, she thought. And evidently, a place for Richard Blackthorne to hide.

No wonder he was feared, whispered about. The mansion towered over the village like a landed lord, high on a green mound of earth and surrounded by a seven-foot-tall stone wall, the sea as its moat. And from her room at least, it possessed a magnificent view of the river and the islands beyond. Flawlessly peaceful. She lifted her hand and shielded her eyes, staring at the house, at the tallest tower peaking the mansion. For a second she saw a figure at the window, the stark white of his shirt against the dark curtains, then he was gone, receding into his cave of stone.

A lonely dragon-prince, she thought, who did not want to be rescued.

TWO

She should have just called in the grocery order, Laura thought, and kept filling the shopping cart, ignoring the people staring at her, the young men, much younger than she would *ever* consider dating, leering at her. Yes, she decided, that one was definitely a leer. She smiled sweetly, the parade smile, she thought with a sadistic little chuckle. A couple of the men were fishermen, covered in fish guts and wearing rubber boots. Stunning.

She checked her list, then headed to checkout. Here it comes, she thought, noticing how everyone in the immediate area approached slowly, like stalking cats. A teenage boy swept his broom a little nearer. The cashier looked eager despite the crowd of people waiting. Customers stared openly. No wonder Blackthorne never came out of his home. Whatever happened to southern hospitality?

"You're new here," said the cashier, a blonde wearing too-big earrings and sporting a mouthful of gum that was well beyond ladylike.

"Yes. This is a lovely island." Make them prod, she thought.

"You stayin' at the castle on the point?"

Like there was another house designed like a castle on the island? "I'm Mr. Blackthorne's nanny."

"Nanny!" several people exclaimed at once.

Laura glanced around, making eye contact with each person. "Mr. Blackthorne is expecting his daughter to arrive, and I am here to care for her."

"Oh, the poor child," an elderly woman said, her accent heavy and drawn.

"Why?" Laura asked, yet knew the answer.

"To have such a horrible man for a father."

"You've met Mr. Blackthorne, then?"

"Not exactly."

She hoped her expression was slathered in innocence. "Then how could you possibly know what he's like?"

"He doesn't leave that place," the cashier said. "He hasn't shown his face in four years, even Dewey hasn't seen him up close and he lives there."

Dewey, she assumed, was the groundskeeper she'd yet to meet.

"He's—he's mangled," the young man bagging her groceries stammered.

"And if you've never seen him, then how do you know that?"

The kid shrugged as if it was common knowledge. Yet no one had seen Blackthorne.

"I fail to see where looks matter." She tried controlling her temper, hating that appearances were such a priority. She understood, for she'd experienced reactions to her own appearance, albeit the complete opposite. Women refusing to befriend her, believing she was a snob and thought she was better than them. Or men tripping all over themselves to impress her, each trying to get her into their bed or something as superficial as having her on their arm for some social function. An impression to be made. A trophy. Not one person, not even her former fiancé, had seen beyond the face God gave her. And apparently no one wanted to see beyond Blackthorne's scars, either.

It all made her stomach twist in knots that were achingly familiar. Her defensiveness, for a man she did not know, and for herself, reared along with her temper.

"Charge his account and have them delivered by three," she said, and left, aware of the stares boring into her back.

She skipped the cab ride back, and let her temper cool with a walk through the quaint little town, but the memories came, of her mother pushing her into TV commercials even as a child, the pageants that only invited viciousness. She had hated all of it. And when she was old enough, she chose the ones she wanted to enter. A bit hypocritical, granted, but then, she'd wanted to go to college and she'd needed the prize money and scholarships.

She glanced around at the shop fronts, gleaming glass windows, darling porches, white wood benches placed here and there, and tourists and islanders strolling and shopping. Two elderly men sat near the pier swapping sea stories and whittling. From the pile of shavings at their feet, it looked like a daily ritual. And it made her smile and remember her grandpappy rocking on the back porch, carving wooden animals for her and her brothers to play with since they could afford little else. Simple pleasures for a simple life, grand-pappy always told her, and memories of his love lifted her mood.

She drew in a deep breath of the cooling sea air. October was still warm when the sun was up, but during hurricane season the rain came often, the cloud cover making the air overly humid and the island breezes adding to the chill. She wrapped her arms around her waist and quickened her steps down street after street, where the houses thinned to the long stretch of road leading to Blackthorne's house. Even more isolation, she thought, and rushed inside the warmth of the house.

After putting on a pot of coffee, she was rubbing the chill from her arms when she heard the distinct sound of someone chopping wood. Frowning, she went to the back door, brushing back the curtain covering the small window. Everything inside her that claimed her a woman jumped to life as her gaze moved over the bare-backed man swinging an ax, muscles rippling as he split a log with one swipe.

Blackthorne.

Oh, Lord, he was magnificent-looking, wearing nothing but jeans and boots, and from this angle she could barely see his profile. Obviously the unscarred portion, but what she could see of his face was sharp and aristocratic. Dark hair blew in the wind, fluttering at his nape, overly long and shaggy. His arms were ropy with muscles as he positioned another log, lifted the ax and brought it down again, neatly splitting the log and sending the two pieces of wood flying out. He cut two more, then paused in his work, the ax head on the stump and his arm braced on the handle. When he looked off and spoke, she realized he was not alone, and she moved to the window. Another man, older, sat on a bench, playing mumblety-peg with a pocket-knife. Dewey Halette, she realized, and apparently he was more than just the groundskeeper. He was Black-thorne's friend, perhaps his only one.

Dewey spoke to Blackthorne, his animated features beneath the ball cap weathered as a wrinkled apple and tanned as rawhide. His dark T-shirt hugged his taut stomach, the knees of his jeans were worn to white. Her gaze shifted between the men, and as if Blackthorne knew she was there, he kept his back to her. Yet she glimpsed shiny scars marking his rib cage, like long daggerlike slashes. It must have been horri-bly painful, she thought, then wondered again over the specifics of his accident. Suddenly he threw his head back and laughed, the rough sound carried on the wind and startling her with a burst of warmth. At least he was not totally lost to the simple pleasures, she thought, and quelled the urge to join them. If he wanted her to see him, he would have shown himself first off.

He said something that made Dewey blush and the older man stood, shooting Blackthorne a grin, then smugly dumped another stack of unsplit logs at his feet. Blackthorne worked, splitting log after log as Dewey gathered and stacked. Then Dewey stilled, looking past Blackthorne and directly at her.

She stared right back.

But it was Blackthorne who threw down the ax and reached for a hooded jacket.

She stepped out. ''I apologize,'' she called out. ''I didn't mean to intrude.''

"You did," Blackthorne said, his back to her as he slipped on the jacket.

"Forgive me, I'll go elsewhere."

Richard sighed, wanting to turn around and look her in the eye. "No, I can't have you feeling as if you need to be anywhere I'm not."

"But that's what you want, don't you? You'd rather I not be here at all." She saw his shoulders tighten. "The least we can do is be honest with each other, Mr. Blackthorne."

Richard pressed his lips into a tight line and sighed. "Yes, we can. I will tell you that I don't care that I no longer have the run of my own home."

"You don't have to hide."

"I do not hide. I *chose* this lifestyle, Miss Cambridge, and in the last four years, I've learned this is the best way."

"Easiest, you mean."

"Nothing about this is easy, lady."

"What about your daughter? She's expecting her daddy. She needs comforting. She's lost her mother, for pity's sake."

Richard's chest tightened, and he tried to imagine Kelly's grief and how much he ached to comfort her. "That's why I hired you, Miss Cambridge."

"Don't you even care?"

His spine stiffened. Care? How could he tell Laura that when he'd first learned of his child just a couple of weeks ago, all he'd felt was regret and anger at Kelly's mother for leaving him with his baby growing inside her, for not giving him the chance to even know his child before she stole everything from him. His love for his wife dissolved when she'd taken hers away like a punishment and sentenced him to this prison. And now he was to forget the past? "Yes, I care, but forgive me if fatherhood does not spring to life in me. I've barely grown used to the idea." He strode off toward the garage.

"Well, get used to it," she snapped at his retreating back. "The day after tomorrow she will be here, wanting to see you, and just how am I to explain that her father doesn't want to meet her?"

He kept walking, leaving boot tracks in the sod. "Tell her the truth, Miss Cambridge," he called out. "Her father does not want to be another source of nightmares for her."

That left her stunned, and before she could respond, he was out of sight. She turned her head to look at Dewey. "That didn't go very well, did it?"

Dewey studied her slowly, assessing and judging in one sweep, and Laura didn't know how she came out in that contest. His expression revealed nothing.

"No, ma'am," he said.

"I'm Laura Cambridge."

"Mr. Blackthorne said as much."

"What else did he tell you?"

Dewey's expression shuttered, and he turned away to gather logs and stack them between two trees. The pile had to be thirty feet wide and five feet tall already. They probably needed the wood for heat when the power went out during storms. The stone house, she imagined, would get damp and cold.

"Everyone in town believes a totally different story about him, but then, you knew that, didn't you?" She admired the fact that the older man kept Blackthorne's secrets, even at his own expense.

Dewey positioned the logs on the pile, then turned back to the stump.

"Will you at least tell me his routine so I don't start another fight?"

Dewey met her gaze and tipped his ball cap back, staring at her for a second. "Nope."

Her eyes went wide. "I beg your pardon?"

"Mr. Blackthorne does as he pleases, ma'am, and if you run into him again, then I 'spect you'll just have to handle him."

"Oh, you're a big help." She threw her arms out and let them fall. "Would you rather see him hide like a mole in this palace—" she flung a hand at the castle "—or actually get to know his daughter?"

He didn't respond, taking up Blackthorne's chore, and Laura realized she wasn't going to get anything out of Dewey. It was clear where his loyalties lay. Yet when he went to raise the ax, her hand on his arm stopped him. She met his dark gaze head-on, and said, "I am not leaving here until I feel Kelly will get good care and absolutely tons of love," she drawled, letting her Carolina accent slide over him and do the job for her. "You hear, Mr. Halette?"

There was a little twinkle in his eyes just then, and though his expression didn't change, he said, "Yes'm. And call me Dewey, ma'am."

"Laura," she conceded, then turned toward the house and added, "I'm having groceries delivered, which means company's coming. So if you've a mind to keep up this pretense, I suspect you'd better wipe that smile off your face."

Behind her, Dewey blinked, fighting an even bigger smile. "Yes, ma'am."

The sweet aroma of something baking drifted up through the house, and with it came a chorus of laugh-

ter. It drew him, though he kept to the old servants'
staircase that had been walled up for years. Hidden
passageways created a maze through the house inside
the walls; the corridors were steep, narrow, and barely
able to accommodate his size. He hadn't been inside
these walls since he'd discovered them, and part of
him loathed that he was in here now. But there were
people in his home, when for years only he and Dewey
roamed the halls. But now she was here, making herself at home, baking in his kitchen. The temptation to
see was as overwhelming as the scent of baking chocolate. Yet it was the laughter that pulled at him. And
he could pick her laugh out of the din of voices.
Bright, clean, unscarred. It did not stun him as much
as he thought, for there was something about Laura
Cambridge that grabbed him in places he didn't want
touched. She defied and rebelled, and the urge to tempt
her to the brink surged in him, yet he suppressed it,
for he knew he had everything to lose if she saw his
face. His daughter depended on Laura being here for
her when he could not.

He stopped at the end of the dank corridor and de-
pressed the spring panel, catching it so it did not swing
open completely. She was at the oven, removing a
cookie sheet, then sliding cookies onto a plate. It was
such a domestic scene, something Andrea had never
bothered to do, but what caught him off guard were
the three people perched on stools around the butcher
table. She brought the cookies to the counter, offering
them to the guests. Guests. In his house. For the first
time. He wanted to be angry. He wanted them gone
for the simple reason that he could not join in. And
seeing her talking so animatedly made his isolation all
the more agonizing and bitter.

Damn, but she was beautiful, and the three men surrounding the counter hung on her words. Then when she went to put a batch in the oven, he noticed them leaning out to get a good look at her behind. Granted, it was a sweet creation, he thought, but why were they really here? To gape at his house, him or at her?

"This is quite a large house," the teenager said. The regular delivery boy, Richard recalled.

"Yes, it goes on forever." She dropped spoonfuls of dough onto a fresh sheet.

"Scary-looking, too," one man said with a glance around.

"I love it. It's big and glamorous. And just the stone and design alone reeks with history from all over the world."

That's exactly what he'd felt when he'd seen it, Richard thought, leaning back against the inner wall to listen.

"Have you seen him?" the grocer said.

"Of course."

"Is it…bad?"

Richard peered, almost breathless as he waited for her answer.

"Not that I could tell."

No lies, no information, and he wondered why she'd done that.

"Then why does he hide?"

"He's obviously a private man, and perhaps it's because he hasn't been well received and…" She paused in fussing with her cookies to glance over her shoulder and Richard saw the heat ignite in her gaze. "I will tell you now that if even one person utters a single derogatory remark to his daughter, well…let's just say my grandpappy taught me how to fire a shotgun and skin my kills.''

Richard smothered a laugh, and when he looked back, the guests chuckled halfheartedly, not sure if she meant what she'd said. As if on cue, they thanked her for the coffee, the grocer telling her to call him if she needed anything, as they headed out the door.

Laura closed the door and turned back to the counter, popping the sheet into the oven and starting on the last batch of chocolate chip cookie dough. She didn't know a child that didn't love them and hoped Kelly would. She wanted the child to feel welcome in this dark house.

Suddenly she sensed she wasn't alone and lifted her gaze. She saw him, wedged between the corner wall and the open pantry door, a broad shadow where she could see no more than angled light across the worn jeans shaping his body up to his hips. How the heck did he get in here without her seeing him?

"I'd like to think my granny's cookie recipe lured you, but I know better."

"Smart *and* beautiful."

Laura felt her feathers rise. Did everyone have to mention her face in the first ten seconds of conversation? "Want a cookie?"

"No, thank you."

"Don't tell me you are the one person who doesn't like chocolate chip?"

"No."

"Aah, you won't come into the light to get one."

Silence.

"What else do you deny yourself because you choose to stay in the dark, Mr. Blackthorne?" With her last word, she tossed a cookie in his direction. His hand shot into the light, snatching it from the air. For a second the signet ring glinted before his arm receded into the dark.

"And what will you deny Kelly?"

"Nightmares, Miss Cambridge."

"Call me Laura. And I think you are simply cheating yourself."

He scoffed, sarcastic. "You know nothing of me, beauty queen."

She slammed the spatula down on the counter. "You're right, I don't. Just as you know nothing of me…beast." She turned toward the stove, removed the sheet, replaced it with another, then set the timer. Laura squeezed her eyes shut, pushing back the memory of haunting betrayal. Beauty queen. Fat lot of good it did her. She couldn't even keep her fiancé with this face, she thought, clenching her fists.

Richard straightened, wondering why she was suddenly so upset. "Laura."

Her name came out in a growl, husky, like whiskey in the moonlight, spreading softly over her, crushing the memories and offering sympathy she didn't want. Men, people, noticed her face, it was only natural. And Richard was definitely a man. What did she expect? "I apologize," she said. "That was terribly cruel."

Richard had heard worse and the barb glanced off him. "I've angered you. Tell me why."

"It's nothing." She busied herself with arranging cookies and covering them with plastic wrap.

"Liar."

"Back to name-calling, are we?" She tsked softly as she turned to the refrigerator, pulled out a cut of meat and vegetables, then tossed them on the butcher table. They didn't know each other well enough to discuss her past, nor was she about to whine over it. She had better things to do with her energy, she thought, placing the meat in a marinade, then popping it back in the fridge. She diced and sliced vegetables, aware of his presence. As if she were standing close to a fire, she could sense the man's heat. "You're staring."

"How can you tell?" Could she see him and just not acknowledge it?

"I can feel it."

Did she know he could sense her, too? "And what does it feel like?" he said.

Laura stilled. His simple words, murmured low, felt as if they were laced with intimacy and asked in the sultry throes of desire. Her heart quickened unreasonably. "Almost like an invasion." She scooped the vegetables into a bowl. "And I don't like it." She covered the vegetables with cold water, then refrigerated them.

"You're a drop-dead gorgeous woman, Laura. What man wouldn't look his fill? Surely you know that."

"Yes, I'm well acquainted with how much people value looks," she muttered as the timer went off.

"So am I," he said bitterly.

"Well then, we have a common ground." She removed the last batch of cookies, putting the tray on top of the stove before she turned back.

He was gone. As if a cold wind blew across her face, she knew he was gone.

"I don't like that, either, Mr. Blackthorne," she shouted into the house.

There was no answer, not that she expected one.

Richard Blackthorne did as he pleased. The rest of the world be damned.

Richard moved down the back servants' stairs, returning his supper dishes to the kitchen. He rinsed and loaded them in the dishwasher, snatching a cookie from the plate left in the center of the butcher table. Munching, he walked through the dining room, intent on the library, yet frowning when he felt the balmy air whispering through the house. He strode into the living room and suddenly stopped short. Every muscle in his body jerked tight when he saw her. She stood on the back deck outside the living room, the French doors thrown open to the breeze. Her hands rested on the rail, and a soft green robe billowed out behind her like a knight's banner as she tilted her face to a moonless sky. Beyond the deck, the sea crashed against the shore. The flood lamps at the corner of the house offered the only light.

Richard swore he was looking at an angel. The wind caught her auburn hair, lifting it with the swirl of drapes hung inside the French doors.

"Isn't this fantastic?" she said.

He stilled, feeling trapped in his own house.

"Isn't it?" she prodded, twisting ever so slightly to look at him.

Richard knew she couldn't see him clearly, with the light behind her. "You like this weather?"

Laura looked back at the sea. In the distance lightning flashed. "This is my favorite time. Storms, bone-shaking thunder, rain."

Richard realized she'd intentionally turned her back, giving him the chance to come near or leave, doing either without her seeing him. The gesture touched him, and at the same time, made him wary. Would she suddenly flip on the switch and go screaming? Yet as he already knew where Laura was concerned, he couldn't resist coming closer.

Slipping onto the balcony, he leaned back into the blowing drapes at the French doors. "Thank you for dinner." She'd left the tray outside his door on a small table she'd dragged up the stairs.

"You're welcome. You don't have to eat up there all alone, Mr. Blackthorne."

"What do you propose? That we dine like civilized folk?"

"Why not?"

"I think you know the answer to that."

"And what am I to say to Kelly? Sorry you lost your mother, and well, you really don't have a dad, just a benefactor."

He winced. "Tell her whatever you think is best."

"I know you care, Mr. Blackthorne. I saw her bedroom."

"Just because I don't want her to see me, doesn't mean I don't want her to be comfortable here. Don't you get it? She's a child. One look at what's left of my face and she'll have nightmares for a week." He shook his head. "I'd rather spare us both that."

Laura stepped closer and saw him stiffen and fold his arms over his chest. The posture was so defensive, she knew he couldn't be reached. Not now. "Do you really think a child will be satisfied with scraps, Mr. Blackthorne?"

"She'll have you."

"I'm a stranger," she whispered.

"And so am I."

Laura snarled with frustration, her fists clenched at her sides. "You are an impossible man."

There was a stretch of silence, and then he said, "I want to protect her."

"Shielding her from knowing you is not how to go about it."

"You're the authority on children?" Disbelief colored his voice.

"I'm not unfamiliar."

"Really."

Damn his judging tone, she thought, and wanted to kick him. "You don't like that other people see only your disfigurement, so you hide it. But you're no better. You see what you want, Mr. Blackthorne. No, I don't have any children, but I wish I did. Yet, I taught embassy school for years and I did minor in child psychology. That should come in handy. That and being the oldest of five. Suit you well enough?"

Angrily, she pushed away from the rail, heading inside, but he caught her arm, pulling her into the dark folds of fabric with him.

"Yes. It suits."

Laura could bearly catch her breath, her heart was pounding so hard. Lord, he was a big man, his fingers wrapping around her upper arms completely, and as the curtains whipped around them, she felt enveloped by his nearness. His scent and the sudden danger of being in the shadows swirled around her like a silken rope, trapping her with him. The strength of his legs pressed against hers, the heat of his body driving away the night's chill.

He was entirely too mysterious, entirely too intoxicating.

Yet it was not his loneliness, nor his bitter remarks

that drew her. It was the man, the one who'd suffered and survived. The one who dared not let a single soul close to him again. Protecting them as he protected himself.

She saw the shadow of his head ducking toward her and knew he wanted to kiss her. She almost wished he would.

"You smell like...freedom," he whispered, every cell in his body screaming he was a man and she was a soft, beautiful woman. And how long it had been since he'd felt like this, wanted like this.

Even as alarms went off in her head, even as Laura considered she was here, available, and this was likely the first physical contact Richard Blackthorne had had in ages, she was helpless against her need to touch him, and she lifted her hand, laying it on the center of his chest.

His sharp indrawn breath was loud in the stretching silence.

Richard reared back, suddenly aware of what he was doing. "I don't want your pity and this is wrong."

He set her back, almost thrusting her from him, and she stumbled as he rolled around the door frame and disappeared into the house, back to his cave.

She wanted to tell him that just then, in his arms, pity was the last thing she was feeling. The very last.

Three

———

He was a fool.

As stupid as they came.

His wife leaving him hadn't taught him a damn thing, obviously, or he wouldn't have touched Laura. Sitting at his desk, the dawn breaking behind him, Richard punched the keys, made a half-dozen mistakes, then shoved the keyboard away. Leaning back into the leather chair, he closed his eyes and could almost feel the imprint of her body against his again, the soft yielding femininity he ached to explore.

What man wouldn't, he thought. Her body was full and shapely, and she had a walk designed to make him insane. And not only was touching her definitely unwise, thinking about it was going to send him over the edge. He shook his head. This was going to be tougher than he'd thought, and he knew the memory of touching her was as haunting as the real thing.

She was the nanny, he reminded himself. The hired help.

He scoffed and left his chair, walking to the window. Help, my eye. She was every man's dream. And she would be here for a long time, tempting him.

Behind him, his e-mail pinged, his fax machine whined, but Richard ignored it all, gazing down at the endless stretch of beach below. Dainty footprints marked the sand close to the road, and he knew they were Laura's. Would she take Kelly on walks, looking for seashells? Would Kelly even like it here? Would she like her room, the toys? Or would she be overwhelmed and scared? The questions pounded his brain, and he admitted he didn't know a thing about raising a four-year-old girl. But Kelly was all he had left in this world, and he would do his best, offer all he could.

Except yourself, a silent voice prodded. Guilt swamped him.

What if none of it was enough, and he traumatized his daughter? She was so innocent and impressionable. At the moment, he didn't doubt that Laura would do just fine. The woman was charming, even with that sharp tongue, and he suspected that Kelly would finally have some fun, considering she had likely been passed from friend to friend since the accident. Both he and Andrea had no family. Hell, he'd learned of his wife's death from a uniformed police officer and five days later had learned of his daughter from an attorney, the executor of Andrea's last will. With his permission, Katherine Davenport had rescued Kelly from Child Welfare Services, and they'd made arrangements for a nanny and for Kelly to come here. It was all so cold, indifferent, Andrea hiding his child from him till tragedy struck. But he'd had a lot of time to think about the woman he'd met at a charity ball and married seven years ago. Andrea had been a beauty, like a china doll, fragile, yet during their marriage she'd grown selfish and grasping—loving his lifestyle, he felt now, more than him. She liked the maids and cooks, and the more he gave, the more she wanted. Until he wanted children and to stop traveling. She'd balked and argued till he'd given in. She must have gotten pregnant that wild night on the beach before the accident, he thought. Regardless, when the accident took the good looks he'd won her with, she'd left. He couldn't fault her for leaving. She had been weak, maybe a little immature, but nor was he the same man. Inside or out. Idly he wondered what Andrea had told Kelly about him, then dismissed it. It didn't matter. Releasing a sigh, Richard turned back to the computers, working until a soft voice drawled over the intercom.

"All work and no food makes Mr. Blackthorne a grouch."

Richard shook his head, half smiling. He punched the intercom on his desk. "Did you cook?" His stomach grumbled at the prospect.

"Yup, and Dewey can't even begin to eat it all." There was a pause, and then she said thoughtfully, "Never have been able to scale down my cooking to less than six. Good thing I like leftovers, huh?"

Richard wondered if this woman was ever in a bad mood, and he was thankful she didn't mention last night. He didn't want her thinking he was some rutting stag stalking her. Nor did he want her pity. He'd had enough of that from his ex-wife. That and her cringing when he so much as reached for her. He shook his head over what an idiot he'd been last night, but a part of him wanted to know if she'd felt as much heat as he had. Not even Andrea could generate a fire in him like that, and he had loved her.

"I am hungry."

Laura tried not to like the sound of his voice so much, nor remember how it seduced her senses in the darkness last night. Ten times till Tuesday, she'd asked herself how she could be so attracted to a man she hadn't seen, yet she knew that looks, money or charm had little to do with anything the body had to say. And Richard Blackthorne's body said a lot. Laura wished hers would just forget how to listen.

"I'll bring it up," she finally said.

He hated that he was marooned up here. "Thank you," he replied.

A moment of silence, and then she said, "I got your e-mail, by the way. The *rules*."

"And I know you have a comment to make," he said to the speaker on his desk, and could almost see her lips pull into a tight line.

"Are any of these negotiable?"

Ever the diplomat, he thought. "Such as?"

"This one about not going to the third floor. How is the maid supposed to clean?"

"She knows the rules. She lets me know before she comes up and I simply move to another part of the house," he explained.

"I see." Her sigh drifted through the speaker. "This intercom thing is so impersonal."

"It's the way it must be, Laura."

Below in the kitchen, Laura banged her forehead lightly against the wall. Stubborn man. "Nothing is written in stone, then?"

"No." A pause and then he asked, "What do you want, Laura?"

His irritation was like a flag going up. Want? She wanted normalcy. Normal before Kelly arrived. But she knew Richard would fight her every step of the way. "Oh, nothing," she said sweetly. "I will find a way around your rules, you know. Especially this one about not walking through the house at night. I like the night. I like to drink hot chocolate in the dark, look at the stars."

"Then you should feel right at home here."

"Yes, actually, I do."

Richard needed her to feel welcome, and with Kelly arriving in the morning, he was desperate for her to remain, especially since Katherine Davenport had called this morning and said she couldn't find a qualified replacement soon enough. Richard decided that she was mad at him and wasn't looking hard, anyway.

A few minutes later a knock rattled the door and Richard stepped near, peering through the peephole. She certainly was persistent.

"Leave it there."

She stuck her tongue out at the door.

"Charming, Miss Cambridge," he said dryly.

Laura smiled weakly and set the tray aside. "Mr. Blackthorne, about last night…"

Richard groaned to himself and tapped the intercom beside the door. "It was wrong of me to touch you."

"Why?"

He blinked. "You're my daughter's nanny."

"And convenient, huh?"

"*What?*"

She winced at the bite in his tone. "Well, I'm here and a woman, and—"

"Terribly easy on the eyes."

Her lips twisted into a bitter line. She almost wished she was scarred like Blackthorne. At least she'd know men wouldn't want her for just her looks. "That's not what I meant."

"Wondering how long I've been without a woman?"

The husky drawl of those words weakened her knees. "Of course not!"

"Liar."

She folded her arms over her middle and glared at the door. "Name-calling is a childish defense."

"Sorry."

"Forget I mentioned it."

"I will."

"Fine." But she didn't trust that. Especially when he kept the world at arm's length, then suddenly grabbed her last night as if she were a lifeline on a sinking ship. Yet she could not ignore the electricity she'd felt then, the heat jumping through her. And the need to touch him, to feel the hardness of his tall body. He made her feel small and defenseless and in those few seconds, cherished.

It was not something she could easily forget.

"If you want seconds, just holler," she said, and her steps thumped down the staircase.

Richard took the tray inside and gaped at the monstrous amount of food: eggs, pancakes, bacon, sausage, coffee, toast, jam, hash browns and even grits. He was going to have to run an extra mile for this, he thought, and sat down to enjoy it. And not think of the woman who'd prepared it.

Contact between them was minimal for the rest of the day, and Richard had waited impatiently for night to fall, for shadows to envelop him and give him freedom. He felt like a damned vampire; the night was his friend, although it was the daytime and the sun he loved.

Now he stared down at the woman sprawled on his sofa, asleep, an open book on her chest. He tilted his head to read the title. *Children and Grief.* It hit him again how much Kelly would rely on her when he wished it was him she would turn to for comfort. But he'd only make it worse for her. God, he wanted to hold his baby, know all about her, read to her and simply watch her grow and learn. He cursed Andrea again for not letting him share Kelly's life. He realized, with tremendous regret, that he was relying on Laura to love his daughter in his place.

Laura tapped her foot as the ferry docked and the fantail gate lowered. People strolled off the boat, and she searched the crowd for the little girl, for the nurse who would escort her here. What she found was the most beautiful child she'd ever seen, dark-haired and cherub-faced, her hand clinging to Katherine Davenport's manicured fingers.

She met her old sorority sister's gaze and smiled. "I'm glad you brought her."

Katherine glanced down at the little girl and smiled. "I thought someone familiar would be better than a stranger."

Laura could see the question in Katherine's eyes, as to how it was going between her and Richard Blackthorne, and not wanting to give even a hint of last night, she was grateful when a man came up with Kelly's bags. Laura led him to the SUV Richard let her use, and he hefted the cases into the back seat. She tipped him and returned to the pair.

Laura knelt and smiled at Kelly. The little girl buried her face in Katherine's skirts.

"Hi, I'm Laura," she said anyway.

"Hullo," came the muffled reply.

Katherine inched away, forcing Kelly to look at her.

Laura sat on the ground Indian-style as if they had all the time in the world. "Been a tough week, huh?"

"Yup."

"Well I'm going to take very good care of you, Kelly." Still the child looked at her warily. "I promise. I know how to do lots of things. We can play on the beach, ride bikes and maybe even ride a horse."

That perked her up and Laura prayed she remembered how to ride. "Your daddy has three horses, and I don't think they get much exercise, so we will have to take care of them."

"Did you see my daddy?"

The hope in her voice brought a sting to Laura's eyes. "Yes. He's very nice."

"Momma said he was hurt."

"Your mommy was right, he was. But he's okay now." She wasn't about to scare the child with details. "He just doesn't like to be stared at."

Kelly's brows knitted as if she was trying to understand that if he was okay, why didn't he like being looked at. Laura wanted to postpone that meeting till Kelly was settled and feeling safe.

"So, are you ready to see your new house?" Kelly nodded, chewing on the corner of her sweater. Laura reached up and pulled it free. "Speak up, I can't hear your brain's rattle."

The child almost smiled. "Yes, ma'am."

"You're going to love it, Kelly. It's a castle, just like in Cinderella."

"Really?" the girl said.

"Really."

Laura stood and held out her hand. Kelly looked up at Katherine, sighed, then accepted her hand. Laura's heart nearly wept with joy.

"Do you want to come up to the house?" she said to Katherine. "Have some coffee and take a later ferry?" People were already walking past them to get on the boat heading back to the mainland.

Katherine shook her head. "I think it's best if I let you two get acquainted. I'll call you later, sugah."

"I'd like that," Laura said, her gaze direct as she leaned closer and whispered, "since there is nothing temporary about this job and you knew it."

"He needs her in his life, Laura."

"I know, but—" She looked down and found Kelly staring curiously up at them. Laura exchanged a glance with Katherine that said they would take this up later on the phone. Katherine smiled beautifully, then bent to kiss Kelly.

The child wrapped her arms around Kat's neck and held tight for a second. Laura's chest constricted. How frightened and uncertain she must feel, with Katherine as the only familiar face.

Katherine patted her back and whispered that she would come visit soon and that she loved her. Kelly sniffled pitifully and went to Laura as soon as Katherine set her down. Kelly gave Katherine a brave smile, and Laura led the child to the SUV, buckling her into the front seat, then climbed into the driver's seat.

Laura snapped the seat belt and turned on the engine. "Ready?"

Kelly looked up at her with wide blue eyes and nodded, the edge of her sweater caught in her teeth. Laura noticed the sheen of tears and she leaned over, hugging her and whispering, "It will be all right, honey. I know you're scared." Tiny fingers dug into her as Kelly clung tightly.

"I wanna go home."

Laura's eyes burned. She sounded so pitiful and helpless. "I'm going to take you to a new home, and we will have an adventure discovering it all. Won't that be fun?"

Kelly shrugged sullenly, and Laura stroked her soft, shiny hair. They had a long road ahead, she thought, and wondered just how long she was going to be here, and could she ever have the will to leave. For Laura knew, she was already falling in love with the little lost girl.

The instant the house came in sight, Laura heard Kelly gasp with wonder and try to inch up higher to see the place. Motioning her back down as they rode the bumpy unpaved section of road to the house, Laura drove around the back, to the garage, and hoped that the sight of the beach, the stable and huge yard would interest Kelly. It did, especially the swing set and slide that hadn't been there yesterday. She stopped the vehicle, threw it into Park and turned off the engine.

"Go on, go try it out," she encouraged, and Kelly pushed the door open.

Laura rushed around the side to help as Kelly scrambled down and ran toward the gym set. She watched her, her hair wild and flying out in the wind, her little legs struggling to keep up with her burst of energy. The play set was huge, of sturdy wood and rivets, and she smiled as Kelly climbed the slide, slid down, then did it again and again. Laura got tired just watching her, but it was the smile of pure delight on the child's face that struck her hard. How long would it last, she wondered as Kelly tested the glider swing shaped like an airplane, then the plain swing before ducking under the slide to discover the sandbox and toys.

She felt a presence near her and looked up. Dewey strolled close.

"I'll take her bags up," he said, his hand out for the keys. She handed them over. Yet he made no move to leave.

"She looks like him," he said softly. And Laura stared at Kelly, wondering just how much she favored her father.

Suddenly Kelly flew off the swing and raced to her, stopping in front of Dewey and staring at him. Laura realized Kelly thought Dewey was her father. She introduced them and watched the child's smile fall.

"How do, ma'am." Dewey crouched in front of her and his old knees popped.

Kelly looked wide-eyed at his jeans-covered knee-caps. "Did that hurt?"

"Nope, does it all the time."

"My daddy was hurt. Bad."

"Yes, darlin', he was."

"Do you know him?"

"Yes, I sure do."

"Do you think he will like me?" The question came out in a quivering voice, and Dewey exchanged a glance with Laura.

"Yes, princess. He will, very much."

"But where is he?"

Dewey straightened and glanced up at the windows above. "Up there." Kelly walked around him and gazed up at the stone house.

Richard stared at his daughter, instant love swelling through him. He'd watched her play on the gym set, her hair as dark as his, her eyes the same color. She had his smile, too. How hard had it been it for Andrea to look at her every day and see him, he wondered, and moved closer to the window.

Kelly lifted her arm and waved and Richard wanted to rush down there and scoop her into his arms, tell her he loved her and would protect her and was glad she was here. But he couldn't. Still standing back, he waved, his gaze shifting to Laura.

She looked, too, leaning back against the car, her arms folded across her middle. She had a look that spoke volumes, that it should be him playing with his daughter and how could he resist this little girl? Couldn't she see that he wanted to be down there with Kelly? That he wanted to ease his child's pain? That staying away hurt him far worse than it hurt his daughter?

Dewey was already headed inside with the bags, and Laura was saying something to his daughter. And when Kelly slipped her hand into Laura's, he had the urge to pound the windows and howl at his cage. *That should be me.* Kelly was his baby. His.

Laura made lunch for Kelly before they went upstairs to her room because Laura knew the child would have no interest in food once she saw the fantasy her father had created for her. She'd showed Kelly that her room was just across the hall and that she could come to her anytime day or night. It seemed to ease her fears a little. As Laura unpacked and put away her clothes, Kelly investigated the room, and the toys, one large teddy bear with satin mint-green ears and paws holding her interest. The stuffed animal was half her size at least and she dragged it with her from one pile to the next. When she climbed up onto the bed and looked down, she clutched the bear to her chest.

"Scared? Is it too high up?"

Kelly met her gaze. "Nah." She looked around with complete awe, then yawned. "It's so pretty."

"I know, I wish I had a room like this when I was a little girl."

"What kind did you have?"

Laura busied herself with putting away the suitcases, yet said, "It was small and dark and I shared it with my sisters." She didn't mention that the roof was tin and often leaked right on her side of the bed, too.

"Sisters?"

"I have two, but they are grown and married now," she added. They're younger, too, she thought with a little twinge of envy. She'd come close to getting married, to walking down the aisle with the wrong man. A man who wanted her for her face, her poise and grace, she'd overheard him say to his soon-to-be best man. He wanted his *trophy wife* for show—his mistress for his bed.

Laura closed her eyes and willed the humiliation away. Paul was the culmination of a life of judgments. Oh, she knew she'd opened herself up to that kind of appraisal when she'd entered beauty contests, but that was for the prize money for college to get off the farm. Yet she had hoped he'd loved her for more than a pretty face, and when the dream shattered, she'd lost more than just her man. She'd lost some of her self-esteem, too. She'd felt like a piece of flesh bought and paid for, since Paul had showered her with everything a woman would want. Everything except his love.

"Maybe you can meet them. My sister Jolene has a daughter a little older than you." When no response came Laura looked up and found Kelly fast asleep, her head nestled on the teddy bear's tummy. Smiling, she went to her, easing her back onto the pillows, removing her shoes and pulling a comforter over her. Kelly released a deep, shuddering sigh that said it had already been a long day for such a little girl.

Laura brushed a kiss to her temple, switched off the lights, then left the room, closing the door. Outside the door she instantly felt his presence and looked at the staircase at the far end of the hall. She could see his legs from the knees down, his hand on the banister.

"Is she all right?"

"Yes, she's exhausted, though, and sleeping now."

"Thank you, Laura."

"You're welcome. She wants to see you."

"You know I can't do that."

"She needs her daddy."

"Laura…please."

Agony, from denying himself and his daughter, laced his voice and drifted to her. In that instant, Laura realized just how lonely and isolated this man was, and how hard it must be for him to have two women in his house when he'd been free to roam and do as he pleased for years before.

"She's feeling alone and frightened. Everything is new to her, and while that might be exciting, she still only wants to see you."

"Well she can't. I won't scare her more. And I don't know the first thing about little girls and raising them. But you do."

She didn't want to argue, not with Kelly so near. "Well, I won't always be here," she said, then crossed the hall to her room, closing the door.

Richard sighed and rubbed his hand over his face. She would be here, until he decided otherwise, and the thought of Laura leaving made him nervous. He stared down the hall at the floor lights and the door to his daughter's room. He didn't want to chance either female seeing him and getting scared, but the need to be near Kelly was overpowering. He strode down the remaining steps and along the hall. He opened Kelly's door and slipped inside, moving to the bed and gazing down at the sleeping child. She looked so peaceful and innocent. And so little.

He reached, fingering a lock of her hair, then unable to resist, he stroked the backs of his fingers across her cheek. Her skin was soft and smooth, cool to the touch. She was beautiful and his chest tightened. He wanted to scoop her in his arms and hold her.

"Daddy?"

Oh, the sound of that nearly brought him to tears.

"Yes, princess, I'm here. Go back to sleep."

Kelly shifted in the bed, and Richard covered her tiny shoulders, his hand lingering.

"Daddy loves you," he whispered.

And in her sleep Kelly patted his hand. He tensed for a second, the scars on his wrist deep, but she was already back asleep.

Not wanting to chance Laura popping in, he considered taking the passageway, but anger won out. This was his house, damn it. He left the room and was nearly to the third-floor staircase when Laura threw open her door and rushed out. He quickened his steps down the hall, deeper into the dark, and he knew that it would take her eyes a second to adjust as she went from the lighted room to the dark.

"Mr. Blackthorne," she called softly.

His senses instantly picked up her fragrance, warm and spicy and driving through to his skin.

"Mr. Blackthorne."

He stopped. "I'm ignoring you. Walking away. Don't you get the picture?"

"Shh." She rushed toward him. "Of course, I'm a grad-gee-ate and all that," she bit back, laying on the southern accent.

He whipped around. "Not another step."

"What'll you do? Fire me?" she asked, knowing he couldn't.

"There are other ways to make you keep your distance," he said, and watched her disobey and advance toward him.

"Like what?"

"Like letting you see my face."

"Don't think much of me, do you?" she whispered, staring up into the shadows.

Her compassion was there, as was her pity. "On the contrary," he said just as quietly, "I think of you too much."

He took a single step, bringing him dangerously close, and the heat of his tall body instantly penetrated her clothes. She almost swayed against him, it was so powerful and alluring. Her body called out, as if she'd known him in another life, another time. Raw and hungry, and she wanted to know him again. But she couldn't. She'd been used for her looks before, and now here was a man who was holding it against her and using her as a barrier between him and his daughter.

"And it angers you, doesn't it? That it's me here and not someone else?"

"Yes," he hissed, the sound like a serpent warning of a strike. "I see your flawless face, and I feel every scar and gash as if it happened yesterday." His voice lowered, whiskey-rough with a dark yearning for the untouchable. "Then I hear your breath quicken when I am near, feel your body pulse like it is now, and you..."

The words were out before she could stop them. "Makes you feel like a man instead of a hermit."

He froze, every muscle locking hard.

She felt it, like a vise on her bones that made her want to reach for him. "Richard."

That undid him.

And abruptly he turned away and strode up the stairs, to his sanctuary.

The closing door was like a gunshot in the dark, making her flinch, and Laura fell back against the wall, covering her face.

Now she'd done it. He would never come into the light. Not for the desire they shared, or for the little girl they loved.

Four

She felt like pond scum.

Okay, not quite that bad, she thought, stopping in the downstairs hall, her hands on her hips. But bad enough to keep her awake and roaming the huge house at midnight. She wished she'd kept her big mouth shut, that's all. This is what she got from being raised in a house full of kids where you grabbed your chance to talk or were silenced by the din of others. And she wanted her chance to apologize, but Richard wouldn't respond to the intercom or his door.

Fine. She could take a hint. Hardheaded man, she thought, though she knew what he'd said was true. She made him feel things, because living alone in his castle, he'd hadn't had to feel *anything* for some time. Now he had her and his daughter underfoot, and he felt his isolation harder, stronger.

But he made Laura feel, too. Feminine, wanted. And

she realized how much she'd missed that little boost, for no amount of new clothes, bubble baths or chick-pampering had done the trick since breaking up with Paul. Yet being near Richard was unlike anything she'd felt with her fiancé or any other man. Only Richard gave her a rush of sensation, made her heart pound like a hammer, her blood move so swiftly through her veins she felt flushed and warm. Like an internal radar, her every cell jumped to life and screamed with desire when he was near. And he didn't even have to touch her.

Her brows drew down. She wasn't sure if she liked that.

Paul had nearly destroyed her self-confidence, and she'd taken the Wife Incorporated job to get as far away from him as she could. Did she really want to invite anything from such a man again? It was clear that appearances were first in Richard's thoughts. His—and hers. It was that kind of judgment she wanted to avoid.

Sighing, she flipped on a light as she entered the library. Nice. The walls were covered in filled book-shelves, and a sofa and love seat faced each other near the fireplace, a large desk off to the side. A suit of armor rested in the farthest corner like a sentinel to the knowledge one could find here. It was definitely a masculine room, she thought, strolling inside. She smelled tobacco smoke, and just as a shot of panic swept her, she realized it had come from the pipe lying in the crystal ashtray.

Her gaze moved quickly around the room, then to the doorway. "Mr. Blackthorne?"

The thought of seeing him scared and excited her in one breath. No response came, and she picked up the pipe, feeling the bowl. It was only slightly warm and she replaced it, wondering if he had a tweed jacket with leather elbow patches to go with it.

She looked around the room, trying to imagine him here. Was he comfortable surrounded by these books? Had they become his only companions besides Dewey? A rush of pity washed over her, but she fought it, knowing he wouldn't welcome it.

At the bookshelves, she ran her fingers over the titles, slipping one free to read the first page before putting it back. She moved to the desk, sliding into the leather chair and curling her legs to the side. Did he read in here every night? Had she stolen that freedom from him with her presence? Was he that intent on not joining her and Kelly, ever? Laura knew children, and his child wasn't going to be satisfied with this arrangement for long, and she dreaded the moment when Kelly asked to see her father. Just because he was a recluse, he couldn't really expect a little girl to be locked away, could he? How could he expect Kelly to live this way? Well, Laura told herself, she wasn't going to be leaving this castle until she was sure that he and his daughter could find their way to each other.

She rubbed her arms, then stilled when her gaze landed on an array of framed photos on the edge of his desk. She uncurled from the chair, bending over the desk to inspect them, then reaching for the wedding photograph.

"Oh, my word," she whispered, sinking back into the chair. It was Richard, before the accident. "He was gorgeous." His late wife was lovely, pageant perfect, but he dominated the picture. His sinfully dark hair fell down over his brow; blue eyes, so like Kelly's, laughed at the photographer. His features were carved and flawless, aristocratic. He wasn't just handsome, he was downright devastating. Her heart skipped just knowing this man was attracted to her.

Across the hall from the library, in the shadows, Richard rubbed his mouth, her softly whispered words tearing him apart. He'd forgotten about the photo. Since he was in high school, he'd had more women than he could count because of his looks. Until the accident.

His gaze moved to her bare legs as she slung them over the side of the chair. She wore a black scoop-neck T-shirt, and from what he could see, nothing else. His body tightened harder, at her nearness and the knowledge that only a few yards separated them.

But it might as well be miles. If she ever saw his face, she'd know that the man in the photograph died four years ago.

Laura frowned, laying the picture down. Her gaze shifted over the room, to the metal knight in the corner, then to the doorway. A shadow shifted across the wall of the main hall and she quickly left the chair, crossed the room and peered into the corridor. "Come out, come out, wherever you are."

No answer, no one there. Yet as sure as if he was standing next to her, she could feel him.

"Stop this, Mr. Blackthorne," she warned, moving into the center of the hall and searching the dark. "You're only a ghost if you want to be one. If you want to talk to me, just speak up, dammit."

Silence, unending, echoing with loneliness.

"Well, I want to talk to you!"

Movement at the end of the wide hall sent her hurrying after him, and she entered the kitchen in time to see him step outside and pull the back door closed behind him. She rushed to the door, following him out.

"Richard!"

He hesitated for a second, then, fully hooded in a dark sweatsuit, he took off in a run down the beach. She watched until the reflecting designs on his sneakers faded into the dark.

You can't keep in the shadows forever, she thought.

Children were far more resilient than adults, Laura thought.

When she'd expected Richard's daughter to be wary and afraid the next morning, the child proved her wonderfully wrong. Kelly had scampered out of her bedroom and into Laura's with a bright smile and an inquisitive attitude. She wanted to see her new home, play, be a child, and Laura was more than happy to blow off a day's housework and be young with her.

And she wasn't one to just stand by and be an observer, either.

Kelly giggled as Laura struggled to get her legs between the rail guards of the slide. Clearly, she thought, this was not meant for adults. Especially ones with hips. She looked down at Kelly, wiggled her brows, then she scooted off the platform and slid down. Right off the edge and landing on her bottom.

Kelly laughed and raced for her.

"I suppose I'm a little rusty at this."

"Do it again!" Kelly hopped up and down.

"Oh, no, I think you should be the Slide Queen for today," she said, climbing to her feet and dusting off the seat of her jeans.

Kelly was quick to oblige and Laura smiled when she climbed, her short legs barely reaching between the rungs. She slid, launching herself off the end, and Laura wondered if executing a proper landing was something you grew out of.

Kelly went from swing to glider, until she finally lost interest and Laura suggested a walk on the beach. Kelly was racing ahead before Laura had time to snatch up the plastic pail and shovel from the sandbox under the slide. Together they ran down the beach. Hot on her heels, Laura tossed the bucket aside and gathered Kelly off her feet, swinging her around and making her laugh loudly. Well, the tickling could have something to do with it, she thought, loving the little girl's squeals of delight. They plopped down in the damp sand, and though that seemed to shock Kelly, Laura went to work building the moat for their sand castle.

"I'm all sandy," Kelly said when they started back, walking backward to watch the tide erase their creation.

Laura shrugged. "It washes off."

"You won't get mad?"

She stopped and looked down at the little girl, then squatted to her eye level. "Of course not, honey. You can't live at the beach and not get sandy."

"My momma didn't like the sand."

Oh, the poor darling, she thought when Kelly started to cry. Laura pulled her into her arms and stood.

From the distance Richard could see Kelly was upset and crying. His chest squeezed down on his heart as Laura lovingly cradled his daughter in her arms and carried the girl back to the house. His gaze remained fixed on them as they neared, and while he wondered why his daughter was upset, he wanted only to be with them. Jealousy spurred through him as he stared down at them. He hadn't done a lick of work all day because he couldn't stop moving from window to window, drawn by the sound of their laughter.

Laura paused on the front steps, looking up at him. Richard eased back from the window too late. Her expression spoke for her. You should be here, it said before she walked inside.

Laura carried Kelly upstairs, murmuring soothing words as she shuddered with low, painful sobs. Her heart broke for the child, and in her bedroom, she helped her out of her wet, sandy clothes and into a tub of warm bubbles.

A half an hour later, Kelly was clean and sweet-smelling and ready for a nap, although she insisted she wasn't. But Kelly falling asleep facedown in her pea-nut-butter-and-jelly sandwich gave Laura a little hint. She carried the sleepy child upstairs, her tiny arms and legs wrapped around her body, her head pillowed on her shoulder. Laura hugged her warmly, then tucked her in her princess bed. Leaving her with a small light to guard against the darkness, Laura went down to the first floor to clean up the lunch dishes. She prepared a tray for Richard and something for Dewey, then switched on the intercom.

"Lunch is served, *my lord*," she said into the little speaker.

"Thank you."

"I'm not bringing it up. You'll have to risk running into me in the light of day and come down."

"Laura."

"I have work to do, Mr. Blackthorne. Chores I didn't do because I was playing with your daughter."

There was a stretch of silence and then he said, "Why was she upset?"

Laura spared him the whole of it and got right to the root of Kelly's tears. "She misses her mother."

"You seemed to know what to do."

Her heart ached as she remembered Kelly's pitiful tears. "I tried."

"Thank you, Laura."

"You're welcome. She's a lovely child. Now, get your recluse self down here and eat."

"You're being a little tyrant."

She ignored the smile in his voice. "That's me, Laura the Merciless." She clicked off the intercom and took a step away before she turned back and switched it back on. "And when I apologize for last night, I want you in the room when I do it, you hear?"

She didn't respond when she heard him call her name. He was going to come out of there, she thought. If it was the last thing she did, she was going to drag him kicking and screaming back into the land of the living.

Richard heard Kelly's cries, and he could feel them building as he strode quickly down the hall to his daughter's room, tying the sash of his robe. He pushed open the door and focused on the bed, on the child twisting in the sheets and comforters.

The small night-light offered only a pale glow, and her moans exploded in a scream just as he reached her. He gathered her in his arms, whispering that she was safe and he was here. She was stiff and trembling in his arms, her little hands gripping mercilessly at the fabric of his robe.

"Daddy's here, baby, Daddy's here," he whispered, rubbing her back, and when she softened against him, she cried helplessly. His heart constricted in his chest.

"I—I was scared."

"I know, honey, I know."

"Oh, Daddy, Mommy's gone," she wailed pitifully, and he squeezed his eyes shut. How did a four-year-old deal with grief, with a death she didn't understand?

"I'm here now, Kelly."

Her sobs slowly faded, and when her little arms looped around his neck, Richard tensed. She didn't seem to notice the rough scars and he relaxed a little, rocking his child and wanting to never let her go. He wanted so badly to protect her, to climb into her dreams and fight her dragons for her. He had to make her feel safe somehow.

Pressing his lips to the top of her head, he talked to her, telling her how glad he was that she was here, how much he'd wished he'd been in her life before now. She shuddered hard, and even after she fell back asleep, he still held her. This was the third night that she'd had a nightmare. Laura had come to her before him, and Richard wondered why she wasn't here now. Her hearing seemed more acute than his. Exhausted, probably, he thought, laying Kelly down and covering her. Especially after the day they'd had playing on the gym set, and on the beach. And he remembered sitting at the window, watching Laura teach his little girl how to do a cartwheel.

They'd disappeared into the stable after that, and the pair, with Dewey's help, came riding out on the gentle mare. They'd ridden down the beach in a sedate walk, but he could see that Laura wanted to race with the wind. And he couldn't help notice then how close she and his daughter were growing. Richard admitted he was completely jealous, though grateful that the two hit it off so well. Laura would make a good mother, he thought, and wondered again why she wasn't married.

He heard the door creak as it opened. Quickly, he stood, silently slipping into the hidden passageway.

Laura stepped into the room, frowning. She could have sworn she'd heard something. She glanced around, then back at the sleeping child, and bent to brush a kiss to her hair. She inhaled a scent that wasn't Kelly's, wasn't the shampoo she'd used on her hair or the bath soap.

It was…spicy, male, and she straightened abruptly.

"Mr. Blackthorne?" she whispered. She didn't get an answer, but then she hadn't really been expecting one. Even if Kelly was sound asleep, he'd been with her. And that was at least something. He obviously wasn't as distant as he pretended to be.

She left the room, and too awake to fall back asleep, she went downstairs to fix herself some chamomile tea. The halls were dark, the lights running along the floorboards giving off a warm glow as she walked down the back hall and into the kitchen. She was warming water in the microwave when she heard the pop and crackle of burning wood. She rushed into the living room and found a fire blazing in the hearth. He did that, she thought, and slowly she came forward, stopping near the blaze and warming her bare toes. She could feel him behind her somewhere.

"Join me."

She turned. He sat in a high-backed chair, far enough into the shadows that she couldn't see his face. She swore the man knew exactly where every shadow was, how to sit or stand in them so she couldn't see him. It irritated her. Her gaze moved over the maroon silk robe covering his legs, the matching slacks.

"Why aren't you asleep?"

"Not enough activity, I suppose." He brought a crystal goblet of wine toward his lips, into the shadows. The stem glittered as he tipped it. She noticed his right hand was smooth without scars, the other tucked close to his body and out of sight.

"Well, that's your fault. No one is saying you have to stay in the tower."

"I don't want to have this discussion, Laura. Either leave me in peace or join me. There's wine on the sideboard." He gestured with the wineglass.

She hesitated, wondering if it was wise being around him.

"Scared?" he asked, his raspy voice doing strange things to her.

She laughed softly. "Of you? No, your growl is worse than your bite."

"How do you know?"

"Because you won't come close enough to bite," she quipped.

"So brave," he muttered into the wineglass, wishing she'd sit the hell down. The fire cast light through her black satin robe, offering her naked figure in lush detail. He smothered his frustration, yet masochistically couldn't look away. Perfection stood temptingly before him, and the ache in his groin magnified with his anger. He didn't want to desire her, but he was human, no different than any other man. She was a breathtaking beauty with long legs and full breasts, and she was in his house, enthralling him.

"Sit down, Laura," he finally said, unable to stand the sight another moment.

"I'm just going to get my tea." She walked back to the kitchen, prepared her tea and returned. He was still there, and she didn't like how much that pleased her as she sat on the far left end of the couch, close to the fire. She cupped the mug, sipping, staring at the dance of flames. He shifted in the chair and Laura felt it without seeing it.

I hear your breath quicken when I am near, feel your body pulse, he'd said the other night.

Could he feel what he did to her now? Laura took a gulp of her tea, wishing the sensations away, yet they refused to go. She pulled her robe closed at the throat and remembered the photograph. How hard it must be for him, a man who'd made women sigh with his looks, who now felt he'd make them shudder.

She looked in his direction. "I'm sorry for what I said the other night."

"Why? It was true."

His words made her insides shift and burn. "It was rude to point it out."

Richard felt his heartbeat skip. "I accept your apology."

"Thank you, Mr. Blackthorne."

"I think we've wounded each other enough to continue on with first names."

"Oh, Richard," she whispered softly, twisting toward him. "I didn't mean to hurt you."

"The truth stung you more than it did me."

"Stop being so damned cold!" She set her mug down on the coffee table with a thump.

"What would you have me do? Deny that I'm attracted to you? You look like a damned centerfold, for heaven's sake."

"Big deal. My figure is an accident of nature. It's not who I am." She threw her legs off the couch and stood, angered that he could make her feel so much when she'd sworn off men, sworn never to get involved with someone who couldn't see beyond her face, or even try to. "You know what I think?"

"I'm sure you will tell me regardless," he murmured dryly.

She ignored that. "I think you don't trust yourself to test the waters. I think you've forgotten how to act normal instead of like a growling, demanding bear woken from hibernation."

"I know you want that, Laura, but I can't allow it. I won't."

Her hands on her hips, she stared across the room, noticing his fingers clench the wineglass. "And I don't get a vote? Your opinion of me is sinking by the second, I see."

"No, but past experience has taught me well," he said patiently, wishing she was wearing more clothes and not standing near the fire. "I simply hate the way you make me feel."

"Hate? Oh, a girl could just melt over all this praise, Richard. But then, you made your feelings clear the other night. I guess it's good that I'm here only till you can care for Kelly like a real parent." She walked past him.

"Then you will never leave."

That stopped her in her tracks just beyond the chair, and as she looked down at him, sympathy and anger dueled inside her. The fire shone over his dark hair, his broad shoulders, and part of her wanted to sink onto his lap and feel him against her. Another part of her wanted to knock some sense into him. "I can't stay here forever, Richard."

Abruptly he left the chair, moving behind it. "We have a legal contract."

She heard the flicker of panic in his voice and knew she shouldn't have threatened, but he was just so dang stubborn. "Yes, we do," she assured softly, and when she lifted her hand toward him, like a striking cat, he snatched her wrist, holding her back.

"Never try to touch me. That's part of it."

They stood unmoving, and Laura's skin tingled with anticipation. One tug and she could bring him into the light, but she couldn't destroy his trust. He couldn't change overnight. "I'll make a deal with you," she said softly, and felt his finger flex on her wrist. "You don't hold my pageant wins against me, and I won't try to get a peek at you."

He chuckled, and the sound rippled along her spine. "Agreed." He released her.

She nodded, then took a step away, her hand sliding across the top of the high-backed chair, and Richard felt as if it were sliding over him. His fingers tightened on the wineglass, nearly snapping the delicate stem as she walked out of the living room. He couldn't watch.

"One more thing," she said, pausing in the doorway.

He turned. Her back was to him. "Yes?"

"I'm an honest woman. I rarely hold anything back. If you make me mad, I will tell you why, and—" she twisted slightly, looking back at the man in the shadows "—I'm not going to pay for her betrayal...nor her lack of strength."

She was referring to Andrea, and Richard knew she was right. The two women were nothing alike, and yet, even as they antagonized each other in the dark, he never wanted to see her look at him like Andrea had. "You say that when you haven't seen me."

"I don't need to see you, Richard, to know the kind

of man you truly are.'' She walked into the hall toward the staircase, and her bare foot had scarcely touched the first step when he was there, behind her. She froze, not turning around.

The heat of his body penetrated her robe and Laura closed her eyes, waiting. Her knees nearly buckled at the feel of him so close, and she reached for the banister.

"You think I am so honorable,'' he said into her ear, his warm breath sending a shiver down her throat.

"I know you are.''

"Well, maybe you should remember that it's been a while since I've been around a beautiful woman. Hell, any woman.''

"How flattering,'' she whispered, feeling her throat tighten.

"You should be flattered. Because you're the only thing that's ever made me want to come out of the shadows.''

Her stomach fluttered and her mouth went dry.

"Damn it, Laura,'' he said, his voice rough with the same want and need that stormed through her. "When I look at you, all I want to do is to taste you—''

A bolt of pure heat rocketed through her, and she clapped a hand over her wildly beating heart.

"—feel your naked skin under my mouth—''

She swallowed a moan.

"And be—'' his voice lowered to a husky pitch "—deep inside you.''

Five

Deep inside you.

His words evoked images of undulating bodies, of long soulful kisses, and she swayed back against him.

He caught her shoulders, burying his face in the curve of her neck. She shifted into his touch, a tiny fraction of movement that made him tremble. "Oh, Laura," he groaned, her fragrance seeping into him like rain into a dry desert.

She licked her lips, lifting her hand to touch his head, then stilling halfway there. She rolled around, yet as she did, he grasped her wrist, pulling her hands behind her back and locking them in one fist.

The motion drove her body into his, and she inhaled, feeling his thickness taut against her.

"Feel what you do to me?"

She gazed up at his face, hidden in the dark. "It's

no more than you do to me, Richard," she said, her body igniting in ways she never dreamed existed.

His face neared. "Would you do even this without seeing me?" he said, his lips barely brushing hers, enticing her.

Sensation and emotion crackled between them.

"Yes," she whispered.

Instantly his mouth covered hers, a soft molding kiss. Then everything went wild. His mouth slanted back and forth over hers, hard and deep.

And she accepted it, relished the power of it, loving the glorious rush of sensation spilling through her body in a hot wave. Her heart thundered in her chest, against his, and when he fell back against the wall, wedging her between his thighs, she went without protest. It was terribly erotic, the dark stairwell, not being able to touch him when she wanted to sink her fingers into his hair and show him he couldn't control her.

His tongue pushed between her lips, and she opened wide for his invasion, making him moan with unquenched desire, the intimate duel growing stronger and stronger. One hand capturing her wrists, his other sliding to her spine, pressing her into him. She shifted, thrust, groaning with frustration at not being able to touch him.

Richard felt the seams of his restraint threaten to rip open as her tongue swept the line of his lips, driving him mindless with passion. Passion. A once-in-a-lifetime fire. It was as if they were both trying to extinguish it in the single kiss, yet all it did was flame it higher.

His free hand slid up her arm, settling on her shoulder, his fingertips grazing bare skin at the edge of her robe. The simple touch sent a bolt of heat through his body. He squeezed, and she arched into him. He touched her, his hand smoothing down her chest to her breast. Her kiss grew wild, savage, her head shifting back and forth, and she pressed deeper into his long length. He cupped her breast, stroked circles around her nipple as his tongue stroked the recesses of her sweet mouth. Richard felt alive, right here, right now, hot and throbbing for her. He wanted more. Wanted to feel her hands on him, feel her body cradle his, to experience the touch of a woman, this woman. Only this woman.

But he could not. This was all he could have, and when he would rather have stayed right here the remainder of the night, he knew he'd crossed a line he shouldn't have. He tore his mouth from hers.

"No," she cried on a quick breath, and knew he was going to abandon her, leave her like this. Damp and hungry.

"I can't." His lungs working to draw in air, Richard set her back from him and straightened. He released her and Laura staggered back on wobbly legs. He caught her. Her hands rested on his shoulder for balance, and Richard tensed.

"Laura, don't."

She didn't obey. She let her hands slide down his silk-covered chest, feeling his heartbeat thunder beneath her palms, his muscles tense till she reached his robe sash.

Every fiber in him locked tight.

"I didn't do that out of pity, Richard," she said softly. "I wanted it." Her fingertips swept over his waistband, dangerously low, before she turned and walked up the staircase. "Or couldn't you tell?"

Richard stayed there. Because he couldn't move. He

couldn't even form a retort. He watched her climb the stairs, her robe slightly open and exposing a good portion of her breast. She made no move to cover herself as she paused on the first landing to glance into the shadows.

"Do you still hate the way I make you feel?"

He tipped his head back, leaning against the wall. "Yes…and no."

"Which part of you will win out, Richard? The man who just kissed me into heaven, or the beast locked inside?" With that she mounted the steps in a rush, as if afraid she'd come back downstairs and into his arms.

When she was gone from his sight, Richard smacked his fist against the wall, rattling the paintings like she'd rattled him. He'd been a fool to touch her. He was just going to have to stay away from her. But the thought of not seeing her had him aching already.

He'd avoided her for days. Two, to be exact, and it was making him hunger for company. And hearing the rapid pound of footsteps, the squeals of Kelly's laughter wasn't helping. The sound competed with the rain outside. The noise and music and giggling had filtered up to him all day, making him want to steal a peek, but he kept telling himself he had work to do. He glanced at the three computers from which he ran his companies and communicated with his employees, and snarled at them, then snatched up the remote and flipped on the TV. He turned the volume up enough so he couldn't hear the two females playing tag in the house.

Tag. Only Laura would think of doing that, he decided, then realized how well he'd come to know this woman in just a few days. Even as he stared at the afternoon talk show, he thought of how involved Laura was with Kelly, and that she easily devoted herself to his little girl. It wasn't just the laughter and chatter, but little things like the colored ribbons in Kelly's hair that matched her clothes, or the way Laura set a place setting for Kelly with linen and goblets just like Laura's. And how she dropped everything to hold his daughter when she needed it. But he wanted to be doing the holding, the one tying her shoes, wiping her tears.

He switched on the intercom so he could hear the entire house. Odd, to be eavesdropping when for so long there'd been no one to listen to.

"Miss Laura, look!"

He heard footsteps and a moan that was Laura's. That sound—the last time he'd heard it, when she was soft and pliant under his kiss, made his body seize. He rubbed his fingers across his lips, shaking off the memory, and listening.

"Oh, Kelly, she looks so pitiful."

"She'll get squashed if she stays in the stable, won't she?"

"Yes."

"Can I get her?"

"Oh, we just have to. Put on your raincoat, though. Now, you'll have to bend down and be patient. If she comes to you, then you can bring her in. If not, then she's really not ready to be with us and might scratch you."

"Okay," Kelly said, a little sullen. "But she'll come."

Frowning, Richard rose and crossed the upper floor to the far window overlooking the backyard. His daughter ran out, dressed in a yellow slicker, and went to the stable doors. There was a tiny coal-black kitten nestled near the door. Kelly knelt and held out her hand, waiting as Laura had instructed. Richard hit the intercom on the wall.

"A cat, Laura?"

"It's a kitten, and I thought you were working?"

He ignored that and said, "I don't think this is wise. She's only four."

"And she needs something to care for. It will ease the loss she's suffering, Richard. She needs to feel a little in control, and the kitten is harmless."

"Kittens meow at all hours, and it won't eliminate her grief."

"No, it won't. Her father coming out of his cave and being with her is what she needs, but then you won't do that, will you?"

Guilt pressed down on him and he looked at his hand, slashed with scars from the accident. "Dammit, Laura, you know I can't do that."

"No, Richard, I don't know that." Exasperation came through the intercom loud and clear. "What I do know is that you've lumped the reaction of a few onto me and Kelly, and you're cheating yourself out of a lot of love."

Richard rubbed the back of his neck.

"Oh, look! It came to her."

The excitement in Laura's voice nailed him in the chest. "Laura—"

Her voice faded a bit as he heard her say "Walk slowly, honey. It's slippery. Hold her very gently, she's just a baby." She was yelling out the back door. He could hear the hollowness of her voice beneath the slap of rain. Then Laura was close to the intercom, her voice warm but firm. "If you could see her face you would not question this. And I promise, I will see she takes good care of the kitten. It will be my responsibility. Happy, my lord?"

How was he going to fight that and not come out the ogre?

"And I'll make sure the kitten never sees you."

He drew his head back and scowled at the intercom. "Very funny. All right. It's your responsibility."

She clicked off, but he could still hear her voice coming through the speaker on his desk as she helped Kelly off with her coat and wet shoes.

"Oh, isn't she beautiful?" Laura crooned.

"Can I keep her?"

"Of course you can. She needs a home."

"But...what will Daddy say?" Fear laced her voice, and Richard didn't like hearing it. He did not want his baby to be afraid of him.

"Your daddy thinks it's wonderful."

Liar, he thought, and though Richard couldn't see Kelly's smile, he felt it all the way through the house. Laura was determined to make him a hero in his daughter's eyes.

"Is it a her or a him?" Kelly asked in an amazed whisper.

A long pause, a giggle and then she answered, "Yup, darlin', it's a girl."

Three females in his house. A man couldn't win with those odds. Yet he leaned against the window frame and listened, wanting to be a part of it. Wanting to see Kelly's face when she held the ball of fur in her hands. And misery claimed him again.

"She has eyes like you, Miss Laura."

"Oh, I don't think mine are quite that green or that beautiful."

They were, Richard thought. Feline-emerald and mysterious.

"Let's get her warm. Oh the poor thing is shivering. We can go in the living room, and I'll make a fire. You just keep her wrapped in that towel and let her get used to you."

"What do we name her?"

We. She was already attached to Laura, Richard thought, and when their voices faded, he couldn't stay where he was. He had to keep them at least in hearing range. It was bad enough he couldn't see his little girl, he thought, stepping into the servants' staircase, descending.

"…but I've never known a cat that answered to its name, anyway," he heard moments later.

"You've had kittens?" Kelly asked, and Richard slipped out the hidden door and stood in the kitchen, watching Laura build a fire in the hearth.

"Oh, sure, when I was little we always had at least three. And a couple dogs, a goat or two." She flashed the child a smile that sent sparks shooting through Richard's veins. "Cattle, chickens, and lots and lots of peanuts."

"Peanuts?"

"My daddy is a peanut farmer."

Kelly's face lit up. "Does he make peanut butter?"

"No, he sells the crops to the peanut butter makers." Kelly's quick laughter was sweet and filled his heart. "How's that?" Laura asked, nodding to the now burning fire.

"Nice and warm, but the kitty's still shivering."

"Well you just talk to her real soft-like so she gets

used to your voice and knows you won't hurt her. Gently dry her coat, too. I'll go get her some warm milk.''

Scrunched in the corner of the sofa, Kelly beamed up at her. "Thank you *so-o-o* much, Miss Laura.''

"You're welcome, precious," Laura said, and kissed the top of her head.

Laura moved away, pausing at the door to watch Kelly and her pet comfort each other. Animals were one of the best things about growing up on a farm, she remembered.

In the darkened kitchen, the only light coming from over the stove, she opened the fridge, pulled out the milk, then went to the cupboards for a saucer. Her hand stilled for a second as she set the saucer on the counter.

"How long have you been there?'' she said softly, feeling him behind her, on the other side of the counter. In the silence she could hear him breathe. She hadn't been this close to him since their kiss at the staircase, and her insides jumped and tightened at the memory. Dang. She'd hoped time apart would dull the sensations. Apparently all it took was to know he was there to send her body rocketing off in all directions like fireworks set off too soon.

"Long enough to know you're a farmer's daughter.''

Laura laughed shortly as the old joke came to mind. "That's me. Silas Cambridge's oldest.''

"How many kids are in your family?''

"Five. Three girls and two boys.'' She poured milk into the saucer. "We're only a couple years apart.''

"Must have been nice. I was an only child.''

There were times she'd wished she was an only

child, but not many. "It was loud, and cramped, but I wouldn't part with my kin for anything."

He smiled to himself, loving how her roots flowered in her accent sometimes. Her past made him curious. "So, what made you enter beauty pageants, aside from the obvious?"

The obvious. How many times had she heard that? It's *obvious* she's too pretty to do anything more than walk down a runway. *Obvious* that she must be snobby because she's attractive. It's *obvious* men only want her for her face and body. "What difference does it make?"

"I'd like to know more about the woman caring for my daughter, and I'm curious as to how you got from a peanut farm to the State Department."

He had the right, she thought. And if she were a parent, she'd be doing the same thing. "My family is dirt poor," she admitted. "My mother saw that we could make some extra money, so she put me in pageants and commercials when I was no older than Kelly." She shrugged and, with the saucer, turned toward him. "When I was old enough to really understand what a rotten business it was, the vicious competition, I chose which pageants to enter for the biggest prize money and scholarships so I could go to college and get off the farm."

"Admirable."

She scoffed and lifted her gaze. He stood tucked between two open doors, one leading to the front of the house, one leading up the backstairs. She was tempted to flip on the overhead lights. But she'd promised, and Laura Cambridge did not break her oath. Even to the dragon prince.

"Were you trying to escape your roots?"

"Heck, no. I just didn't want to be a farmer's wife with five kids, scraping pennies each month and praying every night for rain so the crops didn't burn in the heat."

The sharpness of her voice startled him.

"I'm sorry—"

"No, don't be." She sighed and held up one hand. "We had it rough when I was younger, but we didn't really know we were poor. Everyone around us lived the same way. Mom and Daddy aren't doing so bad." She made a sound between a laugh and a scoff. "In fact they're doing rather well now. But Mom was so used to not having anything, she still does stuff like save bacon grease and old clothes, can vegetables and make jams, just in case." She shook her head. "Some things you just can't change, I suppose." She picked up the saucer and headed through the dining room to the living room, not sure if he would be there when she came back. Or if she'd come back. She set the saucer on the stone floor, helped Kelly and her kitty to a spot far enough from the fire to be safe, then asked Kelly if she wanted some hot chocolate. The child's smile was answer enough, and as Laura stepped back into the kitchen, she sensed he was still there.

A little part of her leapt with pleasure that he hadn't vanished into his tower retreat. A more logical part of her said she really needed to get a reality check and remember the lessons Paul had taught her about men and their minds.

She found the cocoa packets and warmed water in the microwave. "Would you like some?"

"No, thank you."

How could those three words sound so seductive in the dark? she thought, and could not help but notice how they danced around the fact that they'd come apart like teenagers in each other's arms two nights ago. It was easy to be polite when you're not allowed to look each other in the eye.

Laura cleared her throat as she cleared her mind of the erotic memory. "What about your parents, your family?"

"Kelly is all I have. My parents died six months after each other a year before I was married."

How sad to be so alone, she thought, but knew he wouldn't want her pity. "All the more reason to get to know her, Richard. Soon it will be just the two of you."

Richard couldn't think about that. As far as he was concerned, Laura was staying. And the temptation of her was something he would have to live with and avoid. More so because he couldn't let Kelly see him. He knew his daughter already had an image in her head, and her four-year-old mind could not fathom the damage to his body. She would turn away from him and that was a moment he did not want to experience. Andrea had not bothered to even couch her reaction when Richard's bandages had come off. He could expect no less from a child. Maybe a little more tolerance from Laura. But he would not risk it. Not after he'd held her. Not after a single kiss rocked him to his heels. Her rejection would cut even deeper.

Kelly was his concern, he reminded himself, and not the workings of his body and his need for a woman. It was better to remain in the dark and stay at least three yards from Laura. Any less was dangerous.

"What about your wife's family?"

"Ex-wife," he said. "And she didn't have family, either. At least none she ever talked about."

Laura nodded, curious about the woman he'd married, and not wanting to pry into tender wounds. The way he'd said "ex" spoke of the pain he was still holding, yet he was only hurting himself. The dead didn't care, and Laura decided that only a witch would kick a man when he was down. But no family meant that Kelly would never know what it was like to have grandparents, and cousins. Both of them are so alone without each other, she thought, now even more determined to get him out of the dark and into the light.

She mixed two mugfuls of cocoa, then headed toward the doors to the dining room which led to the living room.

"What made you leave teaching children of foreign dignitaries to work for Wife Incorporated?"

She looked back to where he stood, the setting sun hidden behind rain clouds offering a dark, misty silver silhouette of his tall body. "A man," she said honestly. "A man I truly loved."

Richard felt as if he'd been cut in half with a sword, the anguish in her voice clear and brimming with embarrassment and making him hurt for her. "Oh, Laura, what did he do?"

"Lie, betray, cheat, and the worst, wanted me for just my looks. So you see, Richard, you and I have more in common than you think."

"I don't think so."

"Oh? Don't you want me simply because I'm easy on the eyes?"

"Dammit, there is a big difference. You have no idea what it's like being hideous."

"No, I don't, but I do know what it's like to be judged because of my looks."

Suddenly Kelly rushed into the dining room, making Laura stop. "Are you talking to my daddy? Is he there? Can I see him? Where is he?" She moved around Laura, and when Laura looked into the kitchen, she knew he was gone.

"Yes, honey, it was him."

Kelly looked up at her with wide, forlorn eyes, the kitten clutched under her chin. "Doesn't he want to see me?" Her lips curled down and tears glossed her blue eyes. Laura's heart wrenched and broke right there. Damn him for doing this to his own daughter. "Yes, honey. He does. But he can't, not right now."

"When?"

Sadness crept deep into the single word and made Laura's eyes burn. "Soon," she whispered, yet wondered if Richard Blackthorne would ever come out of his cave to be with his little princess.

Six

Richard had heard the truck, then the doorbell chime, and he wondered why the deliveryman hadn't just left the package on the steps as usual and was now walking around to the rear of his house. Then he understood. Laura. Gossip and rumors in town must be flying over the beauty stuck in the castle house with the ugly beast, he thought with a cynical twist to his lips. He was surprised only one man had come by so far. Richard didn't doubt that Laura Cambridge never hurt for admirers.

But then that's what she'd been complaining of. That men were only interested in her for her looks. Even the man she'd loved. The reason she'd left embassy work. The man who'd cheated on her. Lied to her. And Richard decided this fellow was a complete idiot and not worthy of a woman like Laura Cambridge. She was warm and giving, and deserved a man who appreciated her. He'd seen humiliation in her beautiful green eyes, shame, and an anger that hadn't gone away. How long ago was it? Who was he? For Richard had the urge to bash his face in right now.

Peering down at the yard below, he saw Laura sitting on the picnic table, watching his daughter play on the wooden swing set as she drew something on a child's pad of paper. As the man approached, she set the pad aside and signed for the parcel, then directed him to set it on the back porch steps. But the guy didn't leave. In fact he had the audacity to sit next to Laura. Too close to her, looking at her too intently. Richard ground his teeth when she laughed at something the man said, then gnashed them nearly to powder when she offered him coffee from the thermos beside her. Didn't this *boy* have anything left to deliver? he wondered, irritated.

Dewey came over, and Richard thought his friend's scowl was enough to send the young man running. But it didn't. Laura poured coffee for Dewey, and although the older man swigged his down quickly and gave the guy a glare, the handsome man, at least five years younger than Laura, didn't budge. Richard thought about hurling the window open and shouting at the guy to get going…back to his own family. He was jealous. Insanely jealous. He stepped back and rubbed his hands over his face.

Great.

It didn't seem to matter that he had no right to be jealous of Laura. She wasn't his, only Kelly was, and without Laura he didn't even have that much. He didn't belong. Laura, Dewey, Kelly…they were the family in this house and he was simply a shadow. An echo of a man. God, how had his life come to this?

He'd never thought of himself as a coward, and it went against the grain to be hiding away. Hell, he was doing it for their sakes, though, not his. He didn't want to be the source of nightmares and heart attacks.

A knock sounded, drawing him from his thoughts, and he shifted his gaze from the window to the door behind him. Richard knew it was the maid, Mrs. Coleson. He called out for her to give him a minute, then slipped into the servants' staircase and moved to the second floor. The maid wouldn't be long, since he wasn't a slob. The vacuum echoed in the cavernous house as he wandered the halls, then stopped between Kelly's room and Laura's. He was tempted to slip into Laura's room and look around, but honor squashed that idea flat. He stepped into Kelly's room, making himself busy with checking the structure of the tall princess bed and picking up a few toys. He heard laughter again and went to the window, snapping back the curtain. Kelly was hopping around as her kitten tried to pounce on her sneaker laces. He gripped the curtain fabric in one fist, crumpling the material. He'd give anything to be able to be there with Kelly, laughing. Smiling at Laura. Feeling the sun on his face. Suddenly, Laura twisted, her gaze shooting to where he stood at the window.

And even from this distance, he saw the fury in her eyes. What the hell was she so mad about? She was the one flirting with the deliveryman. The guy followed the direction of her gaze and quickly handed back the cup, tipping his cap before he left.

Laura turned her back on Richard, and said goodbye to the delivery guy, then smiled as Kelly crawled on all fours with the kitten. It was good to see her smile again. She'd been sullen for days after the night with the kitten, the night her father had stood just a few yards from her and still refused to see her. Kelly's feelings were hurt, and when she'd asked why her daddy didn't want her, Laura's fury with Richard grew.

But that didn't stop her from wanting him at the mere sound of his voice.

She had to stop thinking like that, she reminded herself. Paul wanted you for your looks, now Richard does. She held tight to her anger and put a bit of distance between herself and Richard, spending time ordering all the necessities for their new arrival and teaching Kelly how to care for her pet. Now the jet-black kitten sported a new fluorescent-green collar, the tiny bell on it tinkling as she leapt after Kelly's heels. The girl giggled nonstop, taking the kitten on the slide, the animal looking blandly around as if to say, "This is the best you can do to entertain me?"

Their new addition to their strange family now had a name, too, Serabi. She didn't look like a Jasmine, and Bagerah was a boy's name, Kelly had insisted, and since they'd been watching animated movies during the past two days of rain, Laura thought the kitten had gotten off easy. Still, the name sounded so cute coming from Kelly because she had trouble saying her r's.

Laura picked up the lined school tablet again and finished sketching Kelly's pretty face. Art had been a hobby when she was younger, and though she loved creating something from nothing and hadn't lost the knack, she hadn't taken up charcoal or a paintbrush since she'd gone to college. Besides, the maid was cleaning, and she had little to do except love this child, and that came too easily. Laura sighed and paused in her sketching, watching Kelly tuck the kitten inside her jacket. She adored Kelly, her love growing every time the child smiled or crawled onto her lap, or laughed.

That's all you have, a voice in her head whispered. Then why did that past week here feel like more than she'd ever had with Paul? Shrugging off the thought, Laura went back to drawing until the wind picked up, forcing them inside.

Serabi pounced the ground alongside Kelly, but the instant she was inside she scampered off to investigate the million nooks and crannies of the house.

"No, wait," Laura said, catching Kelly before she ran off after the cat. "Wash up first, then I'll fix supper."

Kelly groaned dramatically, then obediently went into the bathroom.

"I'll be inspecting those hands, too, young lady."

"Yes, ma'am," came back to her, and Laura smiled, pulling out a frying pan and the ingredients for her special beef and peppers with angel hair pasta. When Kelly came back out of the bathroom and passed inspection, Laura sent her into the living room to find her pet and watch a video. The click of the intercom, a signal without a voice, was like a cold summons. She turned down the stove and walked to the little speaker fashioned in the wall, and pressed the button.

"You buzzed, my lord?"

"A million comedians out of work and here you are, cooking supper."

She smirked and her anger at him softened a bit. "Amazing, aren't I?"

"What was that deliveryman hanging around for?"

Was that jealousy she heard? "Just being neighborly."

"You or him?"

"A little of both, I 'spect. He's a nice guy, working his way through college for his master's degree."

"I don't care if he's a Rhodes scholar, I don't want strangers around my daughter."

She nodded to herself. "That's understandable. But I think Dewey and I could protect her well enough."

"Think again, Laura. I'm a very rich man, and I wouldn't put it past anyone to snatch my baby and ransom her."

Laura blinked. "Don't you think you are overreacting?"

"No, I do not."

"So what does this mean? No visitors? No outings? Do you really expect Kelly to become a hermit when she has no reason to be?" She jabbed her index finger at the intercom as if she was pushing at his chest. "Well let me tell you, it isn't going to happen! Not as long as I'm around. She needs to go to school, to play with other children. She misses her friends, her old home, and her mother, and frankly, Lord Blackthorne," she snapped, her tone biting, "I'm in charge. And if you don't trust me to protect her, then you get your disagreeable self down here and do it yourself!"

"Now, just a minute…" His voice boomed out of the intercom. "*You're* mad at *me?*"

She leaned closer to the speaker and jabbed the button. "No," she said. "I'm downright furious with you. You hurt Kelly's feelings the other night. You were no more than yards from her and refused to go to her or let her come to you. She's feeling rejected and hurt and—'' she drew in a breath ''—she thinks you don't want her here.''

"What?"

"The mind of a four-year-old. Go figure. She thinks just because you won't see her, talk to her or acknowledge she's here…you don't want her here at all. Strange, huh?''

"Damn.''

"My thoughts exactly. What do you plan to do about it?''

"What can I do?''

"Come down here and face her.''

"Don't you think I want to? But I'll be damned if I'll scare my own daughter!''

"She loves you unconditionally. It's something parents get from their kids without a test, without having to do a dang thing.'' She switched off the intercom and refused to respond for a few seconds. Then she tapped the button one last time. "The ball's in your court. Make the shot or get off the field.''

"What are you saying, Laura?''

His tone was deadly with warning, but Laura butted right up against it. "Stay up there till she forgets she has a father, till she manages to live without either parent. She already is, and it will hurt her less.'' She clicked off and went back to preparing dinner.

Richard called to her twice, but she didn't respond, and he sagged in his leather chair, rubbing his hands over his face, then through his hair. Stubborn woman. Who the hell did she think she was telling him what to do with his daughter? She was just the nanny, for heaven's sake. He set the rules here. Kelly was his child, and he'd raise her as he saw fit.

*   *   *

Richard was tying his tennis shoe when he saw the black paw curl under the door, heard the meow. Pitiful. He rose and crossed to the door, opening it slightly. The kitten peeked around the wood and tipped its head to look up at him. Anybody with a heart would have smiled. The kitten wrapped herself around his ankles, purring softly, and he bent, picking it up. "You are trespassing," he said to the green-eyed animal.

It was late, the house was quiet. Kelly was in bed and he suspected Laura was either in her room or downstairs. He hadn't heard any movement in the house for a couple of hours now. The kitten meowed. Richard spared it a glance, then tucked it against his chest, prepared to take it back to his daughter before his nightly run. But the kitten wiggled her way upward, near his throat, purring warmly and licking his skin. Something skipped through him, the need for contact, for the touch of another living creature, and he rubbed his face against the soft black fur as he crept down the hall. Serabi purred harder.

He stepped into Kelly's room, the night-light a soft glow in the corner. He laid the kitten near Kelly's chest, and watched the little thing paw the blankets, circle, then settle down. Kelly's hand immediately went to the kitten, resting on its back.

She doesn't think you want her here, Laura had said. And since this morning he'd tried to figure out a way to make Kelly understand that she was the best thing to come into his life. That he needed her so badly. Carefully, he sat on the edge of the high bed and simply watched her sleep. The kitten lifted its head and regarded him like an intruder, then lay back down.

Kelly stirred. Richard tensed.

Her eyes fluttered open and he stayed still, his heart pounding. It was dark enough that she could see no more than his silhouette. He didn't want her to think she was being set upon by some ghoulish creature in the dead of the night.

"Daddy?"

He could hear the quiver in her voice and he prayed it wasn't fear. "Yes, princess."

"Are you mad?"

"Oh, honey, no. Why would you think that?"

"You never come see me."

"I'm here now, aren't I?"

A pause, then she said, "Yes, I guess so."

Richard did what he shouldn't do. He reached for her, gathering her in his arms. The kitten protested, and he lifted the animal out of the way and set it on the pillow. Kelly's arms latched around his neck and she clung. His throat tightened and he whispered in her ear, softly, soothingly. "I love you, Kelly. I love you so much. I'm so very glad you are here with me now."

"Really?"

"Oh, yes, baby, of course I am. I love you. I wish I could come outside with you, I wish I could play on the beach with you, but it's just not possible."

"Why?"

"Because…I can't be in the sun." The lie stuck in his throat.

"Do your cuts still hurt, Daddy? Momma said they were deep."

Richard closed his eyes. Deep? They went clear to his soul. "Yes, honey, sometimes they still hurt." In ways he prayed she never learned.

"Oh." She sighed heavily, her body warm and soft

against his chest. "I fell down once and cut my knee. It hurt for a very long time."

Richard felt the back of his throat burn. In her own way she was being sympathetic, trying to understand. It made Richard's heart ache, because she shouldn't have to try so hard. "I was so lonely till you came here, Kelly."

"Me, too, Daddy." Her little arms squeezed, her hand against his torn throat, but she didn't seem to notice. "I love you," she whispered, then yawned.

Unconditional love, Laura had said. And forgiveness? He rubbed her back, rocking her, never wanting to let go of this precious gift. Her arms slackened, and he knew she was falling asleep. He moved the kitten, laid his daughter down and tucked them together. Both yawned adorably.

Richard slid from the bed.

"Don't go yet, Daddy."

He smiled tenderly and whispered, "I won't, honey. I'm right here." He sat in the rocker, taking up a storybook. Kelly's eyes opened briefly, and in the dark, he whispered softly, "Once upon a time, in a land far, far away, there lived a beautiful young girl..."

Beyond the hill, beyond the stone wall surrounding the grand house, Laura stood on the shore, her toes curled in the sand, her hands shoved deep in the pockets of her jacket. She felt bad for pushing Richard, but she never met a man more stubborn than the lord of Blackthorne Castle, she thought with a wry twist of her lips. Moonlight skittered across the surface of the water. The wind whipped at her hair, snapped at her thin cotton slacks, and a shiver pushed up her spine. More rain, more storms, she thought, and reminded herself to watch the news and see if there was a hurricane watch. She glanced back at the house, and saw a figure trotting down the slope from the house.

Richard. He disappeared near the gates, then appeared again on the beach, heading her way in a steady jog. She headed back immediately. He was hooded, his dark sweatsuit making him nearly invisible in the night, the only light coming from the dozens of security floodlights surrounding the big stone house.

When he noticed her, he stopped.

She hesitated for a second, then walked briskly toward the house. "Laura," he said as she passed, not looking at him.

"I don't want her in the house alone."

"The alarms are set."

"That makes little difference if she wakes in the middle of the night and starts wandering around looking for me."

Her, not him, Richard thought, and felt a pang of jealousy skip through him. That's why she was here, he thought. To care for and love his daughter. To do the things he couldn't. "Laura, wait."

"For what? For another argument? You know my feelings."

"Do I? You come apart in my arms one night and the next you want to take my head off."

"With good reason for both," she snapped, and the air between them sizzled. "That kiss in the stairwell has nothing to do with your daughter and how much she wants to be with you."

"I know." He moved closer. "I wanted to make certain you did."

She stepped back. "Let's not talk about it," she said, fighting the ridiculous urge to launch into his arms and kiss him again. How did he do it, she wondered. How did he always manage to find the shadows to stand in?

"That won't make it go away," he said. There was a hard stretch of silence, and she could hear his breathing, the rustle of his clothes in the wind, and then in a low rough voice he said, "And I don't want it to."

Neither did she. Still, though, she had to say, needed to say, "I won't be used."

"I appreciate the glowing vote of confidence. But I'm not the bastard that hurt you."

"That really doesn't come into this. That kiss showed us both how volatile it can get between us." How incredibly exquisite, how wonderful, she added silently. "I'm convenient, and I don't think it would matter who I was."

"Dammit, you only cheapen yourself when you say that!"

"I like the truth. It's easier to swallow."

"Then you're living a lie." Suddenly he stepped forward, looming over her, and this time she didn't back away. "I wouldn't begin to know how to use a woman. I've only loved once in my life." He drew in a long breath and said, "And not one moment of it compares to what I feel when you're near."

Laura felt her knees soften, her heart skip. "It's just lust."

"Lust I know. Lust is just a temporary comfort."

She tried to keep her voice even. "And I'm only temporary in your life, Richard."

"Good God, what the hell did he do to you?" he demanded, hating this cold side of her and needing to know where it was born.

She tipped her chin up. "He proposed, and I made the mistake of saying yes, of believing he honestly loved me. Two days before our wedding, I learned he was marrying me for my award-winning face." Richard groaned in sympathy, but she didn't want pity from him. She'd had enough of that from her friends and sisters. "Paul fully intended to keep the mistress he'd been romping with, after the marriage. I was to be his trophy wife. Smile pretty, be at his side, keep his home, give great parties and produce a couple of heirs." She shook her head, looking briefly out at the sea. "It's so antiquated, it makes me sick. I would have wanted for nothing, though." She looked at him, still always hidden in the shadows. "Except his love."

"He was a selfish, arrogant fool." The man had this beautiful, intelligent woman in love with him and he'd discarded her! A first-class jackass, Richard thought.

"I like to think so." He grasped her upper arms, and she gasped, anticipation she didn't want rocketing through her. "Don't, Richard. I can't get involved with you like that again."

He scoffed. "I think we are well past that. You're living in my house, caring for my daughter…driving me insane." His head descended. "Try again."

He neared, and she inhaled his scent, the heat of his body blocking the wind and warming her skin. Laura couldn't lie to herself. Despite how dangerous this was, that she would get her heart broken again because he chose isolation over coming into the light for his daughter, for her. Despite the fact that she craved his touch as he craved hers. She wanted him to kiss her again, an almost desperate need to know if those moments in the stairwell were genuine, if his touch still held the power to turn her inside out. Or was it all just the mystery of his face and body, his detachment from life, the pain he locked in darkness and turned into himself and let eat at his soul.

Or was it only the erotic lure of a whiskey-roughened voice cloaked in the shadows that was seducing her into this madness?

Seven

Richard tasted her sweetness even before he brushed his mouth over hers. A fractured sound snagged in the back of her throat, a cry for more, a denial of the crackling heat between them. He almost couldn't stand not touching her. His hands flexed on her arms, and she swayed against him.

Then his mouth devoured hers, and heat spiraled through him, around him, sinking into his bones and tearing him in two. "Laura," he murmured, and she whimpered, her fingers digging into his chest, clawing.

"We shouldn't," she gasped, sliding her tongue over his lips, making him groan darkly.

"We are." Her hands crept up his chest, and he caught her wrists, pulling them from him and to the small of her back.

"No," she cried softly, and when he gripped them at the small of her back, Laura's desire spun into anger. "I can't do this," she gasped, tearing her mouth from his. "I can't live like this. I won't. We have nothing if you won't trust me."

She struggled, and he instantly released her. Laura didn't look back as she ran toward the house, her body screaming for his and her heart breaking for them both.

Richard watched her go, trying to draw an even breath. It wasn't happening, his chest tight, his blood singing with desire and his groin throbbing for her. And in that instant, he saw himself as a pathetic parody of who he once was. And he hated it.

After a run that tested his torn muscles, Richard returned to the house, grabbing a glass of water before he went upstairs. Passing through the living room, he found one of Laura's drawings lying on the coffee table. It was a sketch of Kelly sleeping in a big chair with her kitten. Another of his house, another of his daughter on the slide smiling beautifully. What shocked him was that they were not only incredibly good, but that love showed in every line and shadow. And it was done on a child's tablet with a regular pencil. Richard took one of Kelly and headed to his rooms, almost uncaring if he were discovered roaming the halls. And yet knowing Laura would do her best to avoid him.

The next two days proved him right.

Laura left his meals by his suite door with a simple knock and no more than a word or two. She knew if she spoke to him she'd remember too much, want too much. She knew it wouldn't help, but she needed some distance to get her head and heart on the right track. But every time she thought of him, she simply felt confused.

She focused on playing with Kelly, who seemed wonderfully happy today. They'd walked on the beach collecting shells. They washed and dried the shells and glued them to an old mirror she'd found in a box in a garage when she was looking for another pail. The garage was a mess on one side and neat on the other, and Laura realized that quite a few things in those boxes must have belonged to Richard's wife and were reminders of his marriage. She pushed that thought aside.

"Shall we paint it to match your room?" Laura asked, and Kelly shook her head.

"I want to give it to Daddy."

Laura blinked, then smiled. "I bet he will love it."

"I'm going to take it to him."

"Honey, I don't think that would be a good idea." But Kelly was already running into the house, her treasure clutched to her chest. Laura followed her, catching her before she made for the stairs. "Kelly, stop. It still has to dry. Why don't you put it in your room for now."

"No, I want to give it to him!"

Kelly yanked from her grasp and raced for the stairs. But Laura was faster and caught her, holding her tightly.

"Let me go!"

"Honey, you can't see him. No one can."

Kelly cried, and Laura sat on the stairs, holding her, pulling the shell mirror from her clutches and setting it aside. A few shells fell off, pinging on the floor like tacks and Kelly wrapped her arms and legs around Laura and cried as if her heart was breaking.

"What's going on down there?"

Laura didn't respond to the voice on the intercom, instead whispering softly to Kelly, then carrying her and her prize upstairs. The little girl's sobs eased and Laura laid her in her bed, pulling off her shoes. Kelly shuddered and sniffled, and though it was time for her nap, she fought sleep.

"I want my kitty."

Laura brushed Kelly's hair from her face and said, "I'll go find her."

When she left the room, Kelly sat up, then climbed from the bed and pushed her desk chair to the wall. Standing on it, she pushed the buttons on the speaker panel.

"Daddy? I have a present for you. I made it myself. It's a mirror."

He didn't answer.

"Daddy?"

"That's very nice of you, honey. I'm sure it's lovely."

"Don't you want it?"

"Yes, I do, very much."

"Then come get it," Kelly said, a tired whine in her voice.

"I can't, darlin'."

"Yes, you can!" Kelly shouted. "I saw you on the beach. I saw you! You can!"

Laura stepped in, the kitten in her hand. She'd heard enough to know what was going on. Yet Richard's groan of misery slipped through the intercom wires and spilled into the air.

"Come on, precious," Laura said, gathering Kelly off the chair and carrying her to the bed.

Kelly fussed and tears fell. She kicked at the covers and whispered under her breath.

Laura eyed her. "I won't give you Serabi if you're going to be mean."

The little girl sighed and gazed up at her through a curtain of dark hair, her blue eyes sad and forlorn. "I'm sorry," she muttered sullenly.

Laura sat on the edge of the bed, not giving over the kitten. "It's not your fault, honey. I know you're angry that your daddy won't come to you." So am I, Laura thought. "But you have to calm down. I'll give the mirror to him."

"How come you get to see him and I can't?" she wailed.

"I haven't seen him, either."

"But he was in the kitchen with you!"

"It was dark, I didn't see him."

"Oh."

"You take a little nap, and we'll see how you feel afterward. Maybe we'll go for a horse ride."

"Okay." She reached for the kitten.

Laura shook her head. "Serabi is not ready for a nap." The kitten squirmed to be let down, and when Laura set her on the bed, she leapt to the floor and scampered away, proving her point. Kelly looked suddenly very abandoned, and Laura's heart cracked. It wasn't fair, and she couldn't leave her alone right now. She just couldn't.

Laura lifted the child in her arms and brought her to her own bedroom, laying her in the center of the grand four-poster bed, then kicking off her shoes before climbing in. Kelly immediately snuggled into the curve of her body, and Laura pulled a quilt over them. She whispered soothing words, her lips pressed to the top of her head, and together they drifted into dreams, both blocking out the heartache the man in the tower was doling out in spoonfuls.

"I love you, Kelly," Laura whispered.

"I love you, too, Miss Laura," Kelly said, and Laura's sorrow eased.

Richard stood inside Laura's bedroom, watching them sleep. He wanted to crawl into that bed with them, hold them. And he cursed the moment, the decision that had sent razors of glass and metal over his skin, shredding his body as well as his life.

He felt like a chained monster, hurting those he cared about when they dared come within reach. He was so damned grateful for these two in his life, and each day he realized how barren he'd been inside before they came. Emotions were running high in Blackthorne House. He could feel the air tingle with it. And he knew when Laura woke, there would be either silence or harsh words. He wasn't looking forward to either.

He looked down at the mirror in his hand, the border covered in shells of gray, white, orange and rust. There were no mirrors on the top floor. He didn't need them to know what he looked like. He didn't even use them to shave. Yet every time he'd see this one, he'd realize all over again why he stayed out of sight, why no one would want to see his reflection.

But he would keep it, cherish it, and in the glass he'd see Kelly and Laura, tucked together like a mother and daughter, and know he could not truly have either.

He left a note for Kelly, that he had the gift she'd made him, and turned out of the room, Laura's fragrance lingering in the air and clinging to his clothes. Richard walked up the stairs to the tower, closing the door behind him, locking out the world and wishing he could do that so easily with his heart.

The rest of the afternoon went by with the dull pain of a headache. Laura fulfilled her promise of a horse ride and even raced down the beach with Kelly seated in front of her. The little girl loved it and was smiling again. Laura found she had to force her smile.

After a light supper, dishes, a bath and bedtime stories, Kelly was fast asleep, and Laura was alone on the first floor, in Richard's library. She found a box of old photos and papers in the garage, hoping for a picture of Kelly's mother and father to frame and at least give the child some type of connection. Curled in the large leather chair, a glass of wine nearby, she sifted through the piles on the desk. Some were very old, some stuck together because of the humidity and were ruined. Then she found a clear plastic envelope with newspaper clippings. She spilled them on the desk and picked up the largest.

The headline read Entrepreneur Richard Blackthorne Involved in Train Crash.

There was a picture of a car, metal twisted and still locked in the front grate of a train. She could tell a chunk of the car had to be cut away to get him out.

She read the article that told of the crash. A pregnant woman had gone into an epileptic seizure and had been trapped in her car on the tracks. Richard had tried to get the woman out, but the seizure locked her limbs and he couldn't move her. Witnesses to the scene said he'd returned to his car and with his vehicle he'd nudged her compact car across the tracks and out of danger. But not in time for him to get across the tracks. The oncoming train clipped the rear of his luxury car, throwing him into the door, the force driving him through the window. Witnesses said the train continued to drag him and his vehicle for nearly a mile before it stopped.

Laura's hands shook before she finished the article, mostly about Richard's business, his awards and philanthropic donations.

At the bottom was a grainy photograph of Richard before the accident, flawlessly handsome in a tuxedo, and then, beside it as the press was often known to print, was a graphic photo of Richard being loaded into an ambulance. His left side and his head were completely covered. His arm hung limp and was covered with blood, with only his signet ring visible.

Laura picked up another article. Richard Blackthorne in Grave Condition, one headline read. Blackthorne Released from Hospital, Plastic Surgeons Say Damage Is Too Severe. Blackthorne Refuses Interview. There was one about him being awarded by the City of Charleston for his bravery and a picture of the woman and infant he'd saved. Richard's ex-wife accepted the award for him, and her only comment was "My husband's recovery will be slow and hard. He wasn't thinking of the consequences when he came to Mrs. Argyle's assistance, and despite his injuries, he doesn't regret it."

Even on paper, Andrea Blackthorne's comment sounded bitter to Laura. She peered in the box, searching, and on the bottom she found the plaque. *For his selfless act of bravery without regard to his own safety...City of Charleston awards its most favored son...*

A hero. There were more awards and recognition listed in the clippings and not once had Richard appeared to accept them.

Who'd saved these? Because she didn't believe for a second Richard wanted to relive this. She suspected Dewey had and didn't know why she knew that. Andrea Blackthorne had left him after the accident and that told her she couldn't handle the man Richard had become when the bandages had been removed.

She sighed, thinking she might be wrong. Maybe their marriage was on the rocks before, and the accident had been what pushed them further apart. It ticked her off no end that Andrea had left such a mark on Richard that he hid in the shadows. Who's to know what would have become of him if his wife had accepted the results and stood by his side. The darn woman should have been proud of her husband's bravery, his selflessness. She put away the articles, returning her attention to locating a suitable picture or two for Kelly. She found one each of Andrea and Richard, and when Laura stared at his eyes in the picture, she saw Kelly. Does Kelly smile like him? she wondered. She'd only glimpsed the unmarked side of his face once, when he was chopping wood.

Suddenly, the feeling of being watched washed over her. "That's creepy, Richard. Stop doing it. One of these days you're going to scare me, and I'm going to have to hurt you. Where are you?" she snapped when she couldn't find him in the dark.

"Here." He waved, and she saw him near the suit of armor tucked in the corner. It was hard to tell which was man and which was metal.

"Shall I turn out the lights, start the smoke machine so you can hover on the edge of life some more?"

"I see your wit is rapier-sharp tonight."

"Well then, you're not as stupid as I thought."

"What the hell does that mean?"

"Once again I have to tell you when you hurt Kelly."

He winced and pulled a high-back chair into the dark and sat. "You should have helped me out of that, Laura. You know I didn't want to hurt her." His sigh filtered across the room to her, and she felt it coat her with his pain. "God, I can't seem to get anything right lately."

"That's because you still aren't used to anyone intruding in your sanctuary."

"But that didn't stop me from hurting my little girl."

"It wasn't intentional, I know. But I want you to see this for what it is."

"I'm sure you'll tell me, so do go on."

"This routine isn't working and we have to think of something else. Kelly will forgive you, Richard, she already has."

"But a mirror, Laura. For heaven's sake."

Laura blinked. "Oh, God, Richard, I didn't even think of that."

There were mirrors in her bedroom and the bathrooms but nowhere else. Nowhere. "It was just a project for her to do. It was her idea to give it to you."

"I know, I know," he said, regret in his voice. "I have to make it up to her somehow."

"You will." Though she didn't know how. "I read about the accident." She gestured to the clippings.

He tensed. "I don't think I like you nosing in my affairs."

"I could have found it on the Internet easily, you know."

He agreed, but that still didn't make him happy about her looking through his past.

"It was a very gallant and unselfish thing you did."

"I could have gotten us both killed," he growled back.

"On the contrary, your quick thinking under pressure saved lives. One human being hadn't even drawn his first breath. And you gave him that chance and to have his mother."

"He was born a few hours after the accident, I learned."

"Have you seen Mrs. Argyle and her child since?"

He shook his head. "The doctors said she came by the hospital, but Andrea didn't let her in. She wrote to me later. She named the child after me." The baby must be just a few months older than Kelly by now, he realized suddenly.

"Andrea didn't let her in to say thank you?"

"I wasn't in the mood to be very accepting."

"Is that you talking or Andrea?"

"Excuse me?"

His defensive tone was like a red flag. "How did you feel after you woke up from the accident?"

"Glad that I was alive, glad they were alive. I was so doped up with painkillers I don't remember much of the first few weeks."

Moments passed, Laura sipping her wine, Richard sitting in the dark. She could see the outline of the chair, and the lamp on the desk near her offered a pale view of him from the waist down, of dark silk slacks and a robe. His feet were bare and crossed at the ankle. Flawless feet, she thought with a smile.

"How did Andrea feel?"

"She didn't say much."

"I'll just bet she didn't."

"What do you expect? Her husband was mauled by a train for the sake of another woman."

"That's her talking. Don't defend her, Richard. The woman wasn't your mistress, for Pete's sake. You'd have done the same for a man in trouble. You knew what you were doing, it was instinct. Andrea was mad because you'd risked your life and even madder when she saw the results."

A long pause and then he said, "You're right, dammit." The words came on a deep exhale. "I remember her asking how I could do this to her, to us." He scoffed. "It made me see her for what she really was. Then when she brought the best reconstructive surgeons in the country, asking for opinion after opinion when she didn't get the answer she wanted."

"And what was that?"

"...can you return his face to what it was."

Oh, Lord. There was a wealth of Andrea's selfishness in that one sentence, she thought, her heart breaking for him. "Did she leave then?"

"No." He sighed heavily in disgust. "She stuck around for a little while. She slept in the guest room, though, insisting she didn't want to bump into my injuries."

Andrea was probably already showing with her pregnancy by then and wanted to hide it, Laura thought.

"She wouldn't let you touch her, would she?"

He was quiet, tensely quiet, and she could almost feel his shoulders bunching, the wave of humiliation sweeping through him. "No, but I couldn't blame her. Not after I saw my reflection."

"I do."

"Excuse me?"

"If she truly loved you, it wouldn't have mattered."

"I wasn't exactly Mr. Congeniality then."

"You aren't now, so what's the big deal?"

He chuckled under his breath. "There's that rapier wit I love."

That last word made her heart stumble.

"Go on, Laura, I know there is more coming."

"You were in pain, recovering from a terrible trauma. I read the articles. I saw the dates." Her voice tight with fury for the woman who'd taken everything he'd had and left, Laura went on. "It took weeks before they let you out of the hospital, and then you had to have physical therapy, and nurses attend to you daily. From the list of injuries you're damn lucky to be alive." His thighbone had been shattered and was now a steel rod, his hip fractured along with most of the left side of his body. His shoulder socket had been crushed and was now plastic, and there were pins in his arm, fingers and ribs. "Your determination to recover is remarkable."

Richard's head jerked up. Other than his doctors, she was the first person to say that. After the accident and hearing Andrea actually blame him for his own misfortune and what it did to her life, he'd fought back. "I was trying to prove to her that nothing had changed between us," he said into the dark. "After a while I realized it didn't matter. She was already looking at me differently."

"How?"

"Like I was a creature instead of a man."

"Oh, Richard."

Her sympathy cut him in half, made him bleed, but the words came nonetheless. "She slept alone, dined alone, then suddenly one morning I was alone. She couldn't even face me to say goodbye." He crossed his ankle over his knee. "She left me a letter."

How cruel and antiseptic, Laura thought, but kept her opinion to herself.

"I realized I'd probably pushed her to it. No, don't defend me. Please, Laura, don't. I was a golden boy, everything I touched made money. And everyone wanted to be near me." It was as if he was talking about someone he didn't really know. Didn't care to know. "Everyone wanted to be a part of what I was doing at the time. I took it all for granted, the lifestyle, the freedom, the people, and it wasn't until that one moment, when I saw Mrs. Argyle in the front seat of that car, pregnant, struggling for air even as her baby moved inside her, that I realized who I really was. All the rest was just show. That single moment, the decision to push her car across despite the oncoming train…suddenly defined who I was inside. In my soul." He tapped the spot over his heart. "It separated me from the life I'd lived before. It was as if I hadn't lived, really lived until right then. It was the right thing to do," he muttered, as if trying to reassure himself. "It was the *only* thing I could do. And Andrea was cursing me for it with her surgeon's opinions, her repulsed looks she didn't think I saw. And I was angry at the world for showing me a man I wasn't certain I wanted to know."

Discreetly Laura swiped at the tears on her cheek and kept them out of her voice. "What about now?"

"I wouldn't change a thing from that night," he

said, then surprising her, he chuckled slightly. "Except maybe to step on the gas a little harder."

"Yeah well, there is that."

Laura drank the last of her wine, then pushed the rest of the papers and photos into the box on the floor. Richard tensed as she left the chair and walked toward him, her robe molding her slender body.

"Stay back," he whispered harshly.

She didn't, bending into the shadows with him, and he smelled the scent of lemons on her skin, in her hair. "Laura." He was perfectly still, then her hand rose and he caught it. But she twisted and wriggled free, touching the unscarred side of his face, her fingers plowing into his hair, and he groaned softly, a whisper of sound.

"I'm not Andrea, and you're not Paul." Her lips fluttered over his, barely leaving an impression, and Richard fought the urge to drag her onto his lap and explore every inch of her with his mouth and hands. "You don't scare me, dragon. And I'm wondering if remaining a recluse is best for all of us...." She shifted, her mouth near his ear, her words a seductive whisper in the night. "Then why are you always coming so close to the light for me?"

Before he could respond she moved away and slipped into the darkened hall. He knew why. He was beginning to trust her. He told her things he never told anyone. Both were very dangerous moves. Because when he was near her, the last thing he thought about was what he saw in a mirror.

Eight

"**M**iss Laura?" Kelly called from the living room. "What's this?"

Laura dried her hands on a dish towel, slapping it onto her shoulder as she crossed the dining room. She stopped short, blinking at the stack of balsa-wood boxes tied with fat green ribbons.

"Well, honey, why don't we find out?"

She stopped beside the coffee table, looking at the note atop the boxes and addressed to her. She picked it up and flipped the card free. *Show me some more of that hidden talent,* it read. Beside the boxes was one of the sketches she'd done of Kelly, with a note that read *"This is beautiful, you've captured her perfectly. Richard."*

"Whose is it?" the little girl asked, practically jumping up and down in anticipation of presents.

"This note says the top one is for you." Loosening the ribbons, she handed the box to Kelly. The girl immediately plopped to the carpet and opened it, gasping in surprise. Inside were bright beads to string, glitter to decorate with, colored pencils and markers, watercolors, heavy paper. "It's from your daddy," Laura said, and Kelly looked up at her, beaming.

Laura smiled back. Richard had apologized to his daughter the only way he could right now. Kelly asked if she could use them and Laura nodded, turning into the dining room and laying an old cloth on the table to protect it before getting the child a cup of water so she could paint, if she wanted.

Once Kelly was situated, Laura went back into the living room and stared at the boxes. With a sigh, she opened the first and found charcoal paper and all the items she needed to draw. The next box held a fine set of watercolors, complete with palette and brushes, the other held an easel and a collapsible stool she could use outside. And there was another note that read, *"The yellow room in the west wing gets the best light and has a great view of the river and the town."*

Tears burned her eyes. Her throat tightened.

No one had ever taken the time to see past her face to the person inside. No one had bothered to look. Even with her sketches on the walls of her apartment, Paul had not cared or noticed. She'd loved to draw and paint, but had given it up for things she thought were more important at the time. There was a freedom in art that nothing else gave her. Creating something from nothing was a powerful drug. And he'd given it back to her.

"Oh, you got some, too," Kelly crooned, suddenly

at her side and peeking in the boxes. Laura looked down at the dark-haired child, running her hand over the top of her head.

"Isn't it wonderful? We'll have to set up a special place for us to use them, huh?"

Kelly agreed, then skipped back into the dining room to finish whatever she was working on. Laura sat on the sofa, pulled the charcoal set onto her lap and examined each piece, excited about using them and wondering what she'd draw first. She wanted to go thank him now, but she knew he wouldn't see her. Besides, there was still so much to do. After Kelly completed her first picture, Laura proudly taped it to the refrigerator, then herded the child to her bath. It took come convincing because she wanted to try everything right now. But Laura enticed her with what tomorrow would bring, and after her bath and a story, she tucked the little girl in bed. Her child's art set was on the table nearby, as if having it beside her was like being close to her father.

Leaving Kelly's door ajar, Laura paused in the hall, looking up toward the set of stairs at the end of the corridor, wondering what Richard was doing now. She hadn't spoken to him since last night. Or rather he hadn't spoken to her. He hadn't called on the intercom, or appeared out of the shadows as he'd done before. It was as if he'd revealed too much to her last night and wanted distance, another barrier. Yet he'd given her such a wonderful gift. He was a complicated man, she decided, and after a quick shower and dressing in pajamas and a robe, she went downstairs, excited about using the set.

* * *

When Richard heard Laura moving around down-stairs, he stepped into Kelly's bedroom, impatient to be with his daughter. He sat in the rocker, watching her sleep, the moonlight spilling through the windows and bathing his child in silver innocence.

Serabi sat like a jungle queen at the foot of the bed, her forest a mound of blankets.

Kelly murmured "Daddy" very softly, as if she sensed he was there, and he held her hand, his thumb rubbing over the soft flawless back.

"Thank you for the drawing stuff, Daddy." Her eyes never opened.

"I'm glad you liked it, princess," he whispered.

"Miss Laura liked hers, too," Kelly said on a yawn, then quickly drifted back to sleep.

A little jolt of pleasure shot through him just then. He longed to see Laura, talk to her. Being with her was the only time he felt human, that his scars didn't make a difference as to who he was. Biding his time, he picked the book off the nightstand and opened it to the spot he'd marked. He began reading to Kelly, her sleepy smile making him feel like a king.

Richard cursed the size of his own house and strode into the library, stopping short when he found it empty. She was not in her room, not with Kelly, since he'd just left his daughter sleeping soundly. Leaving the library he turned left and headed to the west wing, an unused portion of the house that had been designed for guests and servants. He mounted the stairs, and searched, a needle of panic lacing through him. What if she'd been hurt? He called out for her softly, and when he didn't gain a response he started shoving open door after door.

"Laura!"

"In here."

"Where the hell is here? Damn, this place is like a maze."

Her laugh was light and warm, and still lifting on the air when he opened the door. "You said I could use the yellow room, didn't you?"

Sitting in a chair, she had her back to him, an easel before her, her paintbrush poised on the large sheet of paper taped to a board.

"Didn't you?" She dabbed and swiped.

"I seem to recall that, yes."

"Don't get around the house much, huh?"

"No, not in here. God, I feel like a fool."

"You were worried?"

"Hell, yes. This place is big and old—"

"And always dark," she said, twisting slightly but not looking at him. She stared at the floor just to her left.

Richard realized she was doing that for him, although there was very little light in the room. The curtains were thrown back, and silver beams streamed through the tall windows. "You're painting in the dark, Laura."

"Gee, Blackthorne, you're real quick on the up-take."

He chuckled slightly and shook his head, stepping closer.

Laura felt him moving up behind her, smelled his after-shave, and she wondered when her senses had become so acute. His body seemed to melt through the air between them and press on her skin. The sensation made her aware of herself, of the thin robe and pajamas separating her from him. She longed to see him, not out of some morbid curiosity, but for him to trust her enough to let her that close. All she knew of him was the image of him she'd seen in the photos taken nearly five years ago.

"Isn't it an incredible view?" She gestured to the town spread out like a lady's shirt below, the white-washed homes and businesses glowing under the moonlight, the shore lapping at her sandy hem. Richard's home was on the highest ground, a Machiavellian ogre looming over the village. No wonder everyone was terrified of him, she thought.

"I thought you would like it."

She inhaled a quick breath. He was near.

"But painting without light?"

"It was an image I wanted to catch. The island asleep," she said, then jolted when he put his hands on the back of her chair.

He studied the half-finished painting. "Well, you've certainly captured it," he said.

His voice was near her ear, soft and gentle, as if he were approaching a wild creature.

"The clouds keep moving in and ruining it."

"There's a tropical storm off the coast of Florida. We might get some of it."

"I hope not." She tipped her head a bit, feeling the warmth of his skin so close to her cheek. Her body prickled with new awareness. "The season is almost over."

"Mother Nature can be such a witch sometimes.

But we're safe here. This house has withstood storms for twenty years or so.''

Silence stretched between them, the quiet punctured with only their breathing.

''Thank you for the paints and things. I love them.''

''You're very welcome. You have an extraordinary talent.''

Something curled warmly through her. ''Thank you,'' she barely managed to say, so touched by his words.

''So, beauty queen, was this your talent portion for all those contests?''

She smiled, laughing softly. ''No, it wasn't.'' And why wasn't she offended when he called her beauty queen?

''Not going to tell me, are you?'' She shook her head. ''I like challenges, Cambridge.'' A pause. ''Oh, God, you smell good,'' he groaned.

''Oh, so do you,'' she whispered back, yet when she turned her head, he suddenly moved away, around her and to the window. He kept his back to her, his hands braced on the tall, narrow window frame. Silver light spilled over him, over his dark hair, and Laura was again taken aback by his size. He had to be well over six-foot, and his shoulders blocked the light.

''Good grief, Richard, you're a giant.''

He made a sound, a half laugh. ''Do I scare you?''

''Oh, yeah, can't you see me tremble? You know, you wouldn't be so mysterious to this town's people if you didn't go out of your way to keep them back.''

''They don't come calling.''

''Oh, gee, with the Wall of China around the house, the dragon door knocker to greet them? The house is so isolated, and frankly, Richard, it could use a few flowers or shrubs around those live oaks. Now, I'll be the first to admit that Spanish moss hanging from live oaks is a sight to behold, but it's also scary-looking. Maybe paint the trim a different—''

"Laura."

"Yes?" She drew a quick breath.

"You're babbling." He lowered his arms and turned, leaning back against the wall to the right of the window and facing her. Her heart slammed to her stomach.

She could see his face.

The right side, untouched by scars, and Lord have mercy, he was handsome, hair overlong and gracing the collar of his shirt. A stark white shirt. Always. It was as if he had a stockpile of business suits to get some wear out of. White shirt and dark slacks.

"You cut your own hair, don't you?"

He raked his fingers through it, chuckling under his breath. "I guess even in the dark you can tell."

"I'll cut it for you, if you like. I used to cut my brothers' and sisters'—"

"No, thank you. No one sees it, anyway."

"That's not the point." Laura stood. "You see it. Good grief, Richard..." She stalled.

"What?"

"We can't go on like this. Hiding in the shadows isn't doing either of us any good."

"Speak for yourself."

"What do you gain?"

"My privacy, my dignity. My pride."

She shook her head. "No, you don't. You only keep fresh the wounds she inflicted. Not everyone is like her."

"I am long since over Andrea."

"I believe you, but she's left a mark and I don't like it."

"Too bad," he snapped.

She felt his defenses rising like a wave. "So that's it, right? Come only so close or you'll turn into a snarling beast."

"Don't force this. It won't happen."

"Oh, give it up, Blackthorne! I know who you are, just not what you look like." She took a step. "Let me see you."

"No."

"You've given me a gift more precious than anything I've ever had," she said, gesturing to the paints and art supplies spread over the floor and coffee table. "You've seen *me*. Not the face that won contests. But you won't let me give you anything."

He knew what she meant. To give a promise not to cringe, not to be repulsed. He couldn't risk it. Not when he was just beginning to feel like a man again, not when she made him want to step into the light as much as he needed to breathe in her scent. "You've given me a chance with my daughter."

"And that's enough?"

He didn't answer.

"Is it?"

"No!" he bit out. "Not since you walked through my door."

Her breath skipped up to her throat and she took another step closer.

Richard glared at her, her beautiful face painted in silver moonlight, her long hair waving over her shoulders. Her body hidden in a thin robe and shapeless pajamas. "But it has to be this way."

"No, it doesn't. Not with me."

He closed his eyes and tipped his head back. He clenched and unclenched his fists at his side. Her fragrance wafted up to greet him, entice him, draw on the vestiges of his willpower and threaten to tear it from his grasp. "I have to go. Now."

Laura grabbed his arm.

"Dammit woman, let me go."

Her touch seared through his clothes.

"Why?"

He tilted his head, looking at her. She was inches away. Need raced up his body like ants beneath his skin, tingling and alive. Alive. His chest labored for each breath as if the air had suddenly thinned. He swallowed hard and confessed, "Because if I touch you, I don't think I can stop."

Laura's heartbeat thundered out of control and she lifted her left hand to his cheek, laying her palm to his flawless face. He flinched and she ached for him, for the pain he'd suffered, for the years of seclusion.

"Oh, Laura," he said on a harsh breath, turning his face into her palm, reveling in her touch, her scent. "I can't. I can't. I'll go mad."

"No, you won't."

"Yes," he hissed, folding his hand over hers and kissing her palm, her fingertips, and he trembled.

This strong man who'd survived horrendous obstacles, this man who hid in the shadows for their sake, not his, trembled. It made her feel gifted, cherished, and Laura knew her heart was already deeply involved, her body running a close second and wanting to be first.

She plowed her fingers into his hair, drawing him

down to her. "If you do go crazy, please...take me with you."

In a heartbeat, his mouth was on hers, devouring, penetrating, seething with desire and unhinged passion. He wanted her more than anything, more than his need to be left alone. She opened wide for him, and he plunged his tongue deeply between her lips, tasting again and again. He couldn't get enough, couldn't breathe, couldn't think, only feel, feel when for so long he'd felt nothing but his ugliness. Nothing but desolation. She was a flash of sunshine in his dark life, a lure he couldn't resist, not when she was in his arms, not when she kissed like redemption and madness.

His arm circled her waist, drawing her tightly against him, letting her feel his arousal, what she did to him with only a kiss. He was almost embarrassed at how easily she could arouse him. He drew back for an instant, drawing in a lungful of air, wanting to see her face, her eyes.

"This is not a door we should open."

"Too late," she moaned before she kissed him, pressing herself harder, wedging between his spread thighs. Her left hand explored his throat, his right shoulder, then down to his chest.

He groaned and slid his hand down her spine to enfold her buttocks and mash her to him. The heat of her center seared through his clothes, and he tensed when her right hand skimmed over his scarred shoulder hidden in silk, his chest, then she removed it. He was almost disappointed, yet as the pulse of desire drummed between them, he realized she had her right hand braced at his spine. The caring motion made something shatter inside him. He kissed her harder, tearing at the sash of her robe, spreading the fabric and closing his hand over her breast, feeling her nipple tightening against his palm. He caressed her soft flesh and she purred, pushing into his touch. Then she flipped the buttons of her top. He finished the last two, shoving the fabric off her shoulders and exposing her. His gaze raked her naked flesh as he lowered his head. She leaned back, draped over his arm in open invitation. He closed his lips over her nipple, drawing deeply.

She cried out, a soft breathy sound of pure passion. Her fingertips dug into his shoulder.

He laved and suckled, licked quick, hot circles around her nipple, then devoured her breasts like a starved man at a regal feast. Her flesh tasted of lemons and sweetness, flawless, and the moon's glow scattered over her naked breasts. He raked his teeth across the tender underside, and her breathless pants fueled his desire. And he wanted to give her pleasure, wanted to hear that womanly rush of rapture.

Wanted her.

"I need to touch you. You are so warm and soft. Oh, sweet—" He choked when her fingers circled his nipple. He sank to the carpet, taking her with him and laying her open to his touch.

Laura clasped him to her, his body a shadow against the moonlight spilling down onto them as he kissed her wildly, his head shifting to take more and still more. And she was willing to give.

"Say stop and I will," he said against her mouth.

She drew his hand to her breast. "If you stop now I'll beat you."

He chuckled and took her mouth again, savage and hot, then licked a line down her throat, around her nipples, paying homage to each before moving lower.

Her muscles jumped beneath his touch, and anticipation swept through her as his hand dove beneath the band of her pyjama slacks.

He found her, warm and slick, and he parted the delicate flesh, then pushed a finger inside.

She came off the carpet, her cry pealing around him. She gripped fistfuls of his shirtsleeves, urging him on top of her. He wouldn't go, stroking her harder, deeper, dragging her toward a shattering climax. She undulated with each thrust and draw, gasping, and he savored each sound and scent and touch.

She was a wild creature, telling him how good he made her feel, how much she'd wanted this and wanted him to touch her.

"Come on, my beauty, take it." His lips were near her ear, his words more of a breath than a whisper. "I want to feel you split apart for me."

"I am, I swear," she groaned deep in her throat, riding his hand.

"Not enough."

Suddenly he was off her, and her slacks were gone and he was pushing her thighs apart. He jammed one broad hand beneath her hips and lifted, his mouth covering her softness as his fingers thrust into her. Laura cried out, her hips responding, and heat rose and burned though her, a cyclone of desire pulsing out to her limbs. His tongue circled, his lips tugged and Laura felt the pressure inside her build and build, drawing her tight and hard.

Richard could feel it, the tightening of delicate muscles, the claw of her body desperately reaching for the summit, and he loved it, every sensation she experienced rippling through him and letting him own it. He wanted to be inside her, claiming her, but she could never be his. Never. He couldn't make love to her in the dark, like a prowling creature. She deserved better, deserved more from a man. He could only give her this.

So he did, wrapping his lips around the bead of her sex and sucking gently as he thrust his finger in and out of her body.

It hit her instantly. The wild pump of pleasure convulsing through her and into him. His body flexed as hers did, the luxurious spread of her satisfaction crushing through him and threatening his control.

All she could gasp was "I'm dying," over and over as rapture throbbed through her. The spin and crash of it left her shaking and Laura had barely caught her breath before he was hovering over her, kissing her, his hand still rubbing, drawing out the last pulses of pleasure. She clamped her arms around his neck and kissed him hungrily, ignoring the sudden tensing in his shoulder, ignoring the fact that he clearly didn't want her touching him.

"I want you, *you*."

"No."

"Yes!" She flipped a button of his shirt, slipping her hand inside.

"No." He trapped it, then removed it. "I won't make love to you in the dark. I'd want nothing but light around us then."

"Then turn them on."

Silence.

"You won't come into the light."

He didn't speak.

"I see." She let out a long breath. "Not even for me? Not after doing *that* to me?"

"No."

"I am sick of hearing no, Richard," she said, trying to be calm when her body was still singing, when his hand was still touching her.

"That's the only answer I can give you."

She shoved his hands off and rolled away. "I thought you trusted me. Apparently that just isn't possible." She stood, not bothering to look for her pajama slacks in the dark, and stormed from the room.

Richard sat up, clutching his head in his hands, then plowing his fingers through his hair. Why was the darkness suddenly so much blacker than before?

Nine

Kelly wasn't napping in her bed. Laura had left the child nearly asleep, but when she went to check on her, she was gone.

And she wasn't answering when Laura called out.

Laura opened a door and searched another room, then closed it, moving onto another. She called out to Kelly, but didn't get an answer. They'd played hard all day, more for Laura than the child's sake. She'd needed as much distraction as possible to keep Richard out of her mind. But it hadn't worked. Even after a horse ride, hours on the beach, playing on the swing set, a game of fish with Dewey, and making crafts with Kelly, she could still feel him touching her. Still feel his mouth on her skin. Her body stayed fevered and hungry all day and even a cool shower hadn't changed it.

"Kelly, honey?" she called into an empty room.

The pitch of her voice rose higher and higher when she couldn't find her.

Panic surged through her and she hurried from room to room, then ran to the west wing and found only her paints and easel still where she'd left them. She gave her pajama slacks a disgusted glance, remembering how easily she'd abandoned them to his touch, then snatched them up and went back toward the main hall. She opened armoires and cabinets.

"Come on out, princess. This isn't funny anymore."

She stilled when she thought she heard a sound, muffled and distant, then headed toward it. But she found nothing in the main hall.

Laura hurried outside where Dewey was in the garage, tinkering with the SUV.

"Help me look for Kelly. I can't find her. She must be playing a game or something."

Concerned, he nodded, putting down his tools and searching the grounds as she went back into the house. Through the living room French doors, she looked out over the water and saw no footprints in the sand, nothing leading away from the house. It brought her only a small amount of relief. Where could she be? Why wasn't Kelly answering?

Laura turned into the living room, then the dining room, checking anywhere the child might be able to fit. The broom closet, the bathrooms, calling out to her as she went.

Fear nibbled through her, making her skin flush and her heart pound. Even though the house was secure with state-of-the-art alarm technology, she kept thinking about what Richard had said, that someone could take his child and hold her for ransom. She didn't want to alarm Richard just yet and call him on the intercom.

Dewey stuck his head in the back door and said, "Nope, not a trace of her."

Laura nodded and thanked him, then ran up the stairs, taking two at a time. She hoped Kelly had returned to her room, but it was empty. The crayons and coloring book were still on the table. The bed was still rumpled from her nap.

Laura checked her own bedroom, calling out.

She heard noises from Richard's suite, a thumping sound, and her anger from last night shot through her. She raced up the steps to his suite and pounded on the door.

He responded with a bland. "Yes?"

"Open the door, dammit."

"No."

"I told you I was sick of hearing that! Now, open it or I swear I'll get one of those antique swords and hack through it."

Richard frowned at the door, wanting so badly to fling it open and kiss the woman into a different kind of temper. "Resorting to violence, Laura?"

"I need your help, Richard. Kelly is missing!"

Richard set the barbell on the floor with a thump. "What?"

"She's in the house, I'm certain," she said from the other side of the door. "There are no tracks in the sand and Dewey didn't find her outside, but I can't find her. She was in her bed napping and now she's gone."

"Is the kitten gone, too?"

She frowned. "Yes, as a matter of fact."

Laura heard a cry, soft and muffled. "Oh, God, I can hear her. Where could she be?"

Richard pulled on a T-shirt. "I'll find her."

"How the hell can you find her locked in there? Dammit, Richard, come out! I need help!"

Richard went to the door. "Calm down, darlin'. I'll find her."

His tone soothed and a wave of relief swept her. He would find her. But she couldn't sit still and do nothing. She went to look some more.

Grabbing a flashlight, Richard slipped into the servants' staircase hidden within the walls and walked down one level, then up the opposite staircase on the other side of the house.

"Kelly? Kelly?"

"Daddy?"

"Stay where you are, princess, I'm coming."

"I'm scared." Her kitten meowed.

"I know, precious. Keep talking to me." Richard mounted the narrow stairs. "Can you see the flashlight?"

"No." Panic colored her tone, drawing the one word out.

"It's okay baby, Daddy's here. Nothing is going to hurt you."

"Okay."

Richard smiled to himself. She tried to sound so brave.

He took the next curve, and wished there were lights in the passageways. Half the servants' stairs went to straight walkways, and although he knew the maze in the dark, he realized Kelly could have been trapped in here for days, looking for a way out.

"How did you find the stairs in the walls?"

"Serabi crawled into the corner in my room, then went under the wall."

He must have left it open after one of his late-night visits to her room. Dammit. This was his fault.

"I see the light, Daddy!"

Relief punctured her frail voice, and he heard scuffling. He shined the light down on her, then instantly scooped her in his arms, hugging her tightly. If anything had happened to her... She wrapped her arms around his neck, and he kissed her cheek, rubbing her back. She was trembling and crying her heart out.

"It's okay, baby. Daddy has you now."

"I was so scared," she sobbed.

"I know, baby, I know." He hushed her, soothed her as he carried her back toward the exit. Pressing the wall, the door swung open. He set her down and she rushed out into the upstairs hall.

"Laura, Laura!"

"Oh, Kelly," she cried, and ran down the corridor, sweeping her up into her arms. Laura hugged her and rained kisses over her face. Kelly giggled. Richard stood in the doorway, the light low as he watched Laura with his daughter. Love for Kelly shone in her eyes, glittering in a sheen of tears.

"Oh, precious, I was so worried. Where did you go?"

This was it, Richard thought.

"I was in the walls."

"What do you mean?"

"There is a servants' staircase and passageways leading from this portion, to the west wing," Richard said. "They run all through the house."

Laura twisted, looking in his direction. He filled the

doorway, and with what she could see of him, he was wearing shorts and a black T-shirt instead of his austere crisp white shirt and slacks. Light shone against the twisted muscle of his left thigh and images of last night catapulted to the surface. Her anger slapped them down.

"Passageways?" she said. "And you knew about them?"

"Of course."

"And you didn't think to tell *me?* My God, Richard, she could have fallen! We—I would never have found her. It was selfish and dangerous not to tell me about them!"

"I'm sorry, Miss Laura," Kelly said.

Laura immediately soothed her. "It's not your fault, precious."

"That's how you come to my room, isn't it, Daddy?" Kelly looked between the two, worry in her eyes.

"Yes, princess, it is."

No wonder he could move through the house without detection. Laura let the child down and folded her arms over her middle. "Oh, really."

"Just her room," he clarified, knowing what she was thinking.

She scoffed. "I didn't think you'd come to mine," she muttered. "It has lights in it."

"Daddy reads to me. Every night."

Laura looked down at Kelly. "Wh—what?" She straightened, her arms falling to her sides as she looked at Richard. "You read to her? You come to her room every night through those passageways?"

"Yes."

She marched right up to him and poked a finger in

his chest. "That's—that's…" She sighed, losing her steam and laying her hand to the center of his chest. "That's truly wonderful, Richard. I'm happy for you both."

"It changes little."

"It makes me see that you can manage on your own if I'm gone." He leaned down, and she caught the scent of spice and sweat and man, her senses jolting to life and dancing for him.

"You are not leaving," he growled. He couldn't bear it. Not for a moment.

"Please don't go, Miss Laura. Please!" Kelly squeaked, and the panic in her voice stabbed through her.

"I'm not leaving, honey. Not yet," she said in a lower tone to Richard, and wondered how she could even think of leaving them. "I told you. I can't go on like this."

He bent his head. His mouth a fraction from hers. "But you will."

For Kelly, he was saying, and ignoring the heat of his mouth so close to hers, she knew he was right. Damn him. But that didn't mean she liked his cavalier attitude. "We will continue this discussion later, Mr. Blackthorne." She twisted away and walked to Kelly.

"Yes, beauty, we will."

His words sounded too much like a threat, she thought.

"Are you mad at Daddy, Laura?" Kelly asked as Laura clasped her hand.

"Yes, honey. I am."

"Why?"

"Because he's…stubborn." And prideful and distrusting, and she wanted him to believe in her, trust her—then kiss her into oblivion like he had last night.

"Oh."

Laura smiled to herself. Kelly hadn't a clue and that was just fine. "Come on, honey, enough excitement for one day. You have a nap to finish before supper." Kelly whined her disappointment, but went on to her room, her kitten clutched to her chest. "And as for you, Richard…" she said.

"Yeah," he said calmly, gazing at her behind wrapped in a denim skirt and remembering what it felt like in his hands.

She paused at Kelly's bedroom door, looking back to where he stood, half in the shadows. "Great legs."

A chuckle snagged in his throat, her knowing look speaking volumes, her tone bringing the memory of last night up through his body like steam rising from hot asphalt. His muscles locked, his body screamed for her. He felt as if he were standing before a line drawn in the sand. Loneliness was on one side, surrounding him like a suffocating vapor, and on the other was Laura, hope, freedom and a chance for more.

Laura tossed on the bed, and for the first time in years, the sound of rain and thunder didn't comfort her. She was going to be dragging tomorrow if she didn't get some rest, she thought, and blamed Richard. After giving Kelly her bath and supper, she'd read a couple of chapters of a book, sketched, drunk chamomile tea, but even the relief over finding Kelly and learning Richard had spent time with his daughter every night didn't ease the tension running through her.

She felt on fire. She felt rushed and agitated, and…mad.

At him.

The moments in his arms kept splashing through her like the rain pelting the windows. She threw off the covers and left the bed, crossing to the window. She pushed back the curtain as she sat on the window seat and watched the storm. The water was as black as midnight, waves foaming white. She felt like the sea, alive and beating hard against the shore as if trying to drag them all under and into the darkness.

She glanced back at her robe lying across the chair, wondering if she should go to him and try to convince him to trust her. Then she knew she couldn't. He would when he was ready. If he would ever be ready. If she pushed, she was afraid that he would retreat, and for his daughter's sake, she couldn't risk that. She was here for Kelly, she reminded herself. The child needed her father to be a real dad, to be able to face his own child and the rest of the world without regret.

Part of her ached for the gentle man forced to hide from them. For the man who thought to spare others, when it was himself he spared by remaining in the shadows.

Laura realized how much she cared for Richard. And it scared her. Terrified her because he was a man who held so much in his appearance. She'd been hurt by such a man before, but knew that Paul had wanted her for *only* her looks, only for the picture she'd present to his friends and colleagues.

She and Richard were alike in some ways, she thought. The accident had been a turning point in his life, changing him irrevocably, resetting his priorities. Her broken engagement had made her stronger, made her see once again that there were few people she could trust to be honest with her. To like her for who she was and not what she looked like. Paul had been a life-altering part of her world. A slice of her past she'd learned from and had gone beyond.

Richard thought she was too pretty to want a man like him. But he didn't understand that she didn't see the scars, didn't notice the way he struggled to cover a limp in his stride. She'd fallen for the voice in the dark, the warm kisses that set her body aflame, for the man who was insightful enough to see the artist she'd packed away with her pageant tiaras and gowns.

And she wondered how she could be falling so hard for a man who couldn't trust her enough to let her see his face.

In his suite of rooms, Richard paced like a caged animal. Beyond the walls a storm rolled to life, and he felt each rumble, each flash of lightning as if it ripped through his body. He shoved his fingers through his hair, still damp from his shower, then rubbed the back of his neck. He wanted to go to her, see her, touch her, and yet he knew the danger of it. For both of them.

Last night was proof of that. One touch and he lost his willpower.

She wanted what he couldn't give. To let another human being, besides Dewey, see him. She didn't know what that meant. He'd be throwing himself open to her for her inspection. He hadn't done that for anyone. The risk of it would cost him dearly. And if she turned away from him? Look what he'd have lost. He admitted that his living in the shadows was wearing on him, making his temper short and his need strong.

He missed walking in the sun. Hell, he missed walking into a room with the damned lights on!

He missed her.

Richard glanced at the mammoth arched doorway. The wood thick and carved. The wind howled and the suction in the house pushed against the door, making it jiggle, almost willing it to open on its own. He crossed to it, his hand hovering over the ornate latch.

He stared at his hand, the rips in his skin, and he flexed his fingers.

The he grasped the latch and opened the door.

Laura sat in the window bench, her legs curled to the side. Only one light burned in the far corner of the room, and she realized she'd grown accustomed to the house always being shadowy and dark.

Lightning cracked, the power flickered, went off, then popped back on.

In that instant she knew he was in her room.

Her body quickened with awareness and, wrapping her robe close to her throat, she slowly turned her head toward the doors. "Why are you here?"

"Honestly, I don't really know."

That was fair enough, she thought. "Have a seat." She gestured to the settee.

He took a step toward her, then stopped. "Good grief, it's freezing in here." He went to the hearth, bending to stack logs and kindling.

"I'm not that cold."

"It's damp. You'll get sick. And the power might go out."

He struck a match, the small flame offering a soft glow to his features.

Laura glimpsed the marks slicing his throat. "I could have done that."

"I know."

"Leave, Richard."

"Sick of my company already?"

"Of course not. But you know it's not wise." She drew a long, full breath, then let it out. "I want more than to be touched by you. I want more than simply to be in your arms," she said honestly. "I want all of you."

He stilled, a piece of firewood halfway to the flames.

"Not just the man in the shadows, not just the voice that soothes me and makes me feel alive when you just say my name. Not just the body you never let me touch." She paused, gathering her courage. "I've had half of a man's love and attention before. I've had crumbs...." She swallowed thickly. "I won't stand for that again."

When he said nothing, her heart started to break, pieces chipping away by the seconds.

Then very quietly she said, "We can't share any of it if you won't trust me. It feels temporary. Too much like we're using each other."

"There is more than just sexual attraction going on between us, Laura."

His voice was rough and deep, and Laura's body thrummed with little pulses of heat. Each one growing stronger and stronger as the seconds passed.

"If you know how I feel, if you believe that, then why are you here?"

"I...I had to see you."

"Yet I don't get to see you?" She sighed and willed

back the tears burning her eyes. "Save us both a lot of heartache. Go back to your tower."

Silence, except for the snap and sizzle of burning wood as the flames grew, lighting the room in a deep yellow glow.

He remained before the hearth, on one bent knee, slowly feeding twigs into the flames. The firelight danced and glimmered through his starched white shirt, outlining his shoulders, his chest, and magnifying his size. His shaggy hair shielded his cheek and jaw, curled on his white collar. She wanted to feel it sift through her fingers. Wanted to run her hands over his broad chest, experience his kiss, his mouth on her body. She covered her face with her hands, breathing slowly.

"Please leave," she whispered, her voice wavering with the desire rushing to the surface. With the need for him to trust her.

"No." He straightened, turning toward her, the fire at his back. "Not anymore."

Laura slid her bare legs off the padded bench, her hands clenched on her lap. Her heart pounded furiously.

He clenched and unclenched his hands at his sides.

Richard's gaze moved over her face, and he drank in every nuance, every bend and curve, her beauty classic, her features painfully flawless. Yet poised on the edge of the bench, she looked more like a girl than a woman, her hair falling over her shoulders in a riot of chestnut curls, the thin fabric of her robe hinting at her lush figure hidden beneath.

For a long moment he simply stared, a war raging

inside him, battling with what he wanted, what he could not have, and the choice between.

Richard lifted his hand to her. "Come to me, Laura. While I still have the strength." His hand trembled. "Come see the monster you want to touch you."

Ten

"**Y**ou are *not* a monster." Laura rose slowly, gazing at his hand hovering in the air. His fingers trembled, the sight making her heart break, and she rushed forward, grasping his hand and holding it against her cheek.

"Oh, Laura," Richard groaned.

She pulled him toward her, into the shadows. "In the dark," she whispered, "we are the same. No, shh. I'm not an old beauty queen. You're not scarred. We are just two people, Richard. There are no flaws."

"We can't stay here, and in the light—"

"In the light we are two people with our own imperfections." She lifted her gaze to his, seeing the silhouette of the scars he'd hidden all this time, but nothing clearly. "Show me."

Richard inhaled and exhaled, knowing this was the moment when he'd lose all he'd gained and all he wanted so badly. He turned slightly, facing the fire and bringing her with him.

The light splashed across his face and he winced, yet his attention never left her. He waited. Waited for her revulsion, waited for her features to contort in disgust.

It never came.

Her gaze swept him slowly and Laura felt the tension in him, as if he'd snap in half or bolt for the door, or shove her away. She wasn't going anywhere. He'd found the courage to show her, and she would not fail him. This moment meant too much to her and told her things he couldn't say. And that trust was the greatest gift in her life.

He was a gloriously handsome man still. Just to look him in the eye, into those blue eyes identical to his daughter's, made her heart skip and sputter out of control.

They bored right into her soul.

"You have beautiful eyes," she said. "I feel as if I've waited a decade to see them." For a moment, she simply absorbed the simple act.

Then her gaze moved over the scars.

How much pain he must have been in, she thought. How he'd suffered for that valiant rescue. She reached up, and though he flinched, she pressed her fingertips to the healed wounds.

He slammed his eyes shut, his breathing slow and heavy.

The scars were like the claw marks of a wild animal, curved and even. Two lacerated his forehead into his hairline, one cut across his eyebrow, another the corner of his lid, dangerously close to his eye. More slashed his cheek, down his jaw and his throat before they disappeared under his shirt. He remained perfectly still as she studied each one, a stone statue about to shatter, his arms at his sides, his fists clenched like white knuckled hammers.

Laura's heart broke for him. For the years he'd spent in solitude, believing he was hideous, believing his appearance kept him from being lovable because no one saw the courage it had taken to earn these wounds.

"Look what you've survived," she whispered, awed, and he heard the wonder in her voice.

He met her gaze, watching as she leaned closer. Against his will, his body tensed. "Laura."

"Shh." She slid her hand around the back of his neck, drawing him down. She pressed her mouth to the mark on his forehead, his eyes, his cheek, tenderly, slowly kissing each wound, then prying open the buttons of his shirt and kissing the jagged scars across his throat and shoulder.

He moaned and clamped his hands on her waist and tried to push her away, turn away. "Oh, Laura, don't."

She held him still, understanding his anxiety. "Don't push me away, Richard. Please. You endured this pain when it was fresh. Now it's just scars in your mind." He shook his head, but she kept kissing his healed wounds, opening button after button, laying her mouth over the scars like a soothing balm. "I don't see a disfigurement. I see badges of your courage. Wounds of the war you fought to survive."

Richard's heart beat a steady, hard thud, his hand sliding up her back and into her hair. He gripped handfuls and tipped her head back. "I don't want your touch out of pity."

Her lips curved the slightest bit and she met his gaze

head-on. "Oh, my beautiful beast," she said in a low seductive voice. "The very last thing I feel for you is pity."

His lips curved, then flattened to a thin line. "There are more...my ribs, hip...and leg."

"I don't care. When are you going to understand that?"

"I've never...I mean, no woman has ever touched me."

She smiled softly. "My, my, almost virginal then, huh?"

He choked on a laugh, then went still as glass as she pushed her body into his. He felt every curve and valley of her supple warmth, the firm press of her breast through her robe, and he realized she was naked beneath.

His apprehension slid in a different direction.

Every cell in him screamed for her, his groin thickening with the pulse of his blood. She was madness and freedom and every piece of hunger he'd ever possessed. He whispered her name, his hands charging a wild ride over her spine.

Laura tugged his shirt from his trousers, spreading the fabric and smoothing her hands over the skin she exposed. His body was tanned and tight, the thick, carved muscle wrapping him, telling her that his solitude was spent pumping iron. The result was impressive and she thought he was the most beautiful creature alive. Just the sight of all this man excited her, the feel of him against her driving passion to the surface.

She met his gaze briefly, then closed her lips over his nipple, her tongue circling, and now he trembled. Now he moaned and gripped her tightly. She rubbed his ribs and felt the old wounds laid over heavy muscle.

And with each kiss, Richard felt his soul unwind.

Felt his battered body shout for her, for more.

He thought he'd crumble into dust. And prayed he wouldn't.

He plowed his fingers into her hair, tilted her head and kissed her.

It was an eating kiss. Devouring. Holding nothing back and leaving nothing untouched. His tongue stroked, his lips rolled and tugged. Tasting and taking.

And she gave back more. Always more.

He clamped his arms around her, lifting her off the ground. She was a tiny thing, fragile and lush, and she stole his breath, his soul as they kissed. It wasn't enough.

A desperation raced to the surface, peeling into each other and spilling like hot spiced wine.

"Touch me," she whispered against his mouth. "Oh, Richard, I can't wait."

He did, sweeping his strong hands down her spine, her buttocks, her thighs. Then he hooked his hand beneath her legs and lifted, wrapping first one then the other around his hips.

He sank to the floor on his knees, never breaking his kiss, opening her robe and filling his hands with her naked breasts. She moaned, arching, leaning back like a pagan offering, and he closed his lips over her nipple. She cried out his name, her fingers in his long hair, her hips undulating against his, and he sucked her nipple deep into the heat of his mouth. Then he sucked harder.

Her body tingled in response, wave after wave of pulsing heat engulfing her and spreading outward. Her nerves danced. Between her thighs, she grew damp and throbbing.

The strength of his arousal pushed against his clothes.

And she wanted more. She wanted him inside her, filling her, easing this tight knot working furiously under her skin. Reaching over his shoulder she dragged his shirt up, tearing it from his arms and tossing it aside to the exquisite feel of his mouth and hands on her skin. She molded his chest, his arms, the flat plane of his stomach, her gaze following the path.

"You're so beautiful," she said, and he knew she meant it. Knew that this one woman saw the man and not the scars.

He came unhinged, his breathing labored, his hands impatient as they rubbed over her body. "I'm going to make love to you." There was no question in his voice, no hesitation.

"I was hoping for that."

He peeled her robe off, his gaze raking over her naked body, her thighs bare and spread across his. "This is going to take all night," he growled.

She arched a brow, gripping his belt, flipping it open and sending the zipper down. "I'm not going anywhere."

He swallowed and covered her hand, stopping her. "We need protection."

"I have it covered." She opened his trousers, her smile devilish as she slipped her hand inside.

He clutched her, but Laura explored him slowly, shaping his arousal, feeling him elongate beneath her touch.

A shudder racked his big body. "You're going to make me lose it."

"You said 'all night' and I'm holding you to that."

He pulled her hand free. "Not right this second."

She laughed and brushed her mouth over his jaw, the anticipation of having him, of feeling him fill her, making her eager for more. He laid her back onto the floor, and like a man on a quest, he tasted her body, her breasts, her tight, dark nipples, feeling them peak and harden against his tongue. She purred and let him have his way, and he nuzzled her belly, and when he bent between her thighs, expectation swept her. He parted her, sinking two fingers inside her, and she arched like a cat.

"Look at me," he said, and she did, her eyes opening slowly.

He probed and played, watching her face, her reaction, her pleasure, and with his gaze locked with hers, he scooped her up and covered her softness with his mouth.

She cried out his name in a deep throaty purr, writhing on the carpet. Richard saw every twist and curve of her body, every ripple of her muscles as he tasted her. Then he pushed his fingers deeper, stroked her harder and felt her body paw for more, felt the spin of desire pulsing through her.

It enthralled him. This woman, her taste, the sight and feel of her.

Her pleasure was his. And when she bit her lip and the hot vibration crashed through her, he felt her slick muscles contract as rapture took her.

She stiffened, ground to him, stretched, then curled toward him, reaching for him. "Oh, my heavens!" she gasped. "Richard!" She trembled powerfully and fell bonelessly to the floor.

He chuckled, and before the haze lifted, before she

calmed, he stood and stripped off his clothes. Laura opened her eyes.

He was magnificent, his thighs twisted with muscle, his hips narrow. He stood hard and proud before her, and she rose up on her knees. When he back-stepped, she caught him at the back of his thighs and pressed her mouth to the scar running over his leg to below his knee.

A shiver racked him, and she dragged her tongue higher, her hands moving up and down his thighs.

Then she wrapped his arousal and looked up.

He quaked, and shaking his head, he pried her hand off, sinking to the floor. He pushed her to her back. "Not yet, I need to feel you." He spread her thighs over his, and on his knees, he wedged himself between.

The moist tip of him pushed against her, dipping, retreating, teasing her.

"Come to me now," she said, trying to pull him down onto her.

"I don't want to hurt you."

"You couldn't, Richard. Ever." Suddenly she rose up and climbed onto his lap, enfolding him, guiding him inside her. "I said now."

"Never let it be said I'd deny you," he growled.

She gripped his shoulders, her gaze locked with his as she sank slowly down onto him. Her body shuddered with sensation, her openmouthed gasps spilling against his lips. He was huge and heavy and she pushed down harder.

Brutal tremors racked him, and he wrapped his arms around her, holding her tightly. "Oh, Laura, oh sweet mercy."

"I know," she said, brushing his hair off his face,

holding his jaw, raining kisses over his face. "I know."

It was completion.

It was belonging.

Laura knew nothing would ever affect her more than this moment. Nothing would be more intimate in her life. She'd already lost her heart to him.

Now her soul was joined with his.

His mouth rolled over hers, rich and greedy.

Then she moved.

Richard sucked his breath in through clenched teeth. Laura thrilled at the look on his face as she rocked. His big hands gripped her hips, helping her motion, her slick feminine muscles calling him back.

She was so small in his arms, her slender thighs flexing as she rose and slid down on him. He buried himself deeper with each stroke and, brushing her hair back off her cheek, he gazed into her eyes and knew there would never be another woman in his life. Never be another moment so precious. It wasn't the passion they shared that marked him. It wasn't the desire that stole his control, that made them one. It was her. She reached out when no one would. She opened her heart and mind and gave him salvation with just her smiles. She made him want to be a better man, a father to his daughter. And when he thought himself unworthy, she forced him to see he was worthy. She was more woman than he had a right to want. But she didn't make him feel that way. Never had.

He wanted to roar with the power of it.

And his happiness spilled into his kiss, his need to give her pleasure, make her sob with it. He laid her to the carpet, her thighs draped over his, and he gazed down at her as he withdrew and plunged. Her eyes flared, her smile feline seductive, and he quickened inside her, leaning over her.

Firelight bathed her bare body in brazen gold.

The rain hammered the windows and stone walls.

Neither noticed as he scooped his hand under the small of her back and pushed and pushed, the friction heightening with every stroke, clawing through her body and grasping his in a wet, tight grip. Pleasure skipped over her beautiful face.

"Oh, Richard. Oh—" She bore down on him as the pulses of desire battered her body. Her skin tingled. Pressure built low in her stomach with each push of his body into hers. He bent and gazed directly into her eyes, shoving and shoving, telling her how incredible she made him feel. That he felt like a man again the instant she walked into his home. That he loved her defiance and her mind, and he couldn't bear another moment without her knowing he'd trusted her. And that more, much more than desire brought him here tonight.

He withdrew and plunged. Warm and wet and burning for more.

Scarred flesh twisted over bronze muscle, flexing to the beat of desire and the flawless woman cradling him, smooth and supple.

Yet in the dark their bodies never ended, never began.

In the firelight, inside the castle of stone, was their rebirth.

The storm raged beyond the walls. Thunder cracked white against the black sky as Richard loved her body, pushed into her delicate softness and found hope and freedom and the new hunger for more.

Beneath him, she undulated like a pale ribbon, and he felt her passion unfold and speak to him. Slick muscles clamped him in a velvet fist. She tensed, her fingers digging into his chest as she spread wider, bore harder, and the sight of it pushed him over the edge of control.

He drove into her, pushing her across the carpet. He apologized and she denied it, loving the rawness of them, the energy singing through her. He slammed into her and her breath stalled and rushed. She bowed, locking her legs around his hips as the pulse of ecstasy tore through her.

He threw his head back, a low growl tumbling from his throat, the beast locked inside suddenly set free.

The sound hovered in the air.

He spilled himself into her and Laura felt the throbbing heat of it.

She gripped his hips, grinding to him, pulling him deeper, as if it would never be enough.

He shuddered like a great mountain, his expression strained, and she touched his face, his chest. Then she pulled him down onto her.

The fire hissed and sputtered gently.

Richard struggled to catch his breath. Her hands rubbed over his scarred back, and he cherished the simple motion. He could never get enough of her touch. Never. He brushed his mouth over hers, the back of his throat burning.

And Richard knew that all the pain he'd held, the agony of loneliness that had been his only company, was gone.

In her he'd found the freedom.

And the second beat of his heart.

* * *

For several moments they lay perfectly still.

Then Richard leaned up on his arms and gazed down at her.

Laura smiled, tracing her finger over his mouth, his chin. "Well," she breathed softly, "it's safe to say you haven't lost your touch."

He grinned, a flash of straight white teeth. Her smile widened and she pulled him down for a slow wet kiss.

"Cold?"

"Na-ah," she said, running her hand over his broad shoulder.

"Think the power is out?"

"Who cares?"

He chuckled to himself. "Now I know how to make you lazy."

She opened one eye and regarded him.

"You go a mile a minute, it's a wonder you don't drop dead every night."

"I don't like wasting time."

"Laura…" He hesitated. "I can't tell you what it means to me that you accept—"

She pressed two fingers to his lips. "Don't. I didn't have to accept anything, Richard. I just had to have my curiosity satisfied. It is now and that's done."

His features sharpened.

"You had to do more accepting than me," she said, lowering her hand. "You had to trust me."

Not to be like Andrea, she was saying yet didn't. Laura was right, of course. More than the images Andrea had planted in his mind so long ago had left him tonight. Left when she welcomed him.

Smiling, he rolled to his back, taking her with him. "I want to make love to you in every room in the house."

"Well, you did say it would take *all* night. And it is a very large house."

He chuckled softly and then suddenly he was standing, lifting her into his arms, and when she thought he would move to her bed, he strode to the door. Then down the hall and up the short steps to his suite.

He kicked open the door. "If he has to start somewhere…" He walked to the bathroom. It was huge and rich with deep maroon walls, yet the sound of bubbling water hit her first, then the heat of it as he stepped into the Jacuzzi tub.

He lowered them into the water.

"Oh, my lord."

"It's for my hip and leg. It helps keep them from being stiff."

"There are other things that are still stiff," she said, and under the water she closed her hand around his arousal. He groaned and fell back against the wall of the giant tub. Laura smiled mischievously and slid under the water.

Richard blinked, then seconds later growled loudly, a death grip on the rim of the tub as she took him deep into her mouth. She stroked and manipulated him, then popped up, pushing her hair off her face and smiling.

"You're a witch, a devious, seductive witch."

He grasped her waist and easily lifted her to the edge of the tub, spread her thighs and devoured her.

Her laugh of surprise faded rapidly under the pulse of desire rocketing through her. He pushed two fingers inside, sending hard jolts of pleasure ripping up her body. She gripped his head, feeling raw and savage, and when he flipped her over onto her stomach and positioned behind her, she cried out, "Oh, hurry, please."

And he entered her in one hard push.

She'd never felt anything so wonderful. Hot throbbing desire buffeted her, the pressure tight and hard and building rapidly with each stroke. He gripped her hips and took her higher and higher and he was climbing with her, the intense hardness of him spearing her, and she loved it. Loved his power, the untamed way he made love to her. Then he dipped his hand between her thighs, and she came unglued.

Richard's control slipped as blinding passion tore through him. He wrapped his arms around her, pushing and pushing, his body shuddering violently, sapping his strength. Pure, unfettered pleasure held them enthralled in each other. She shattered beautifully in his arms. Their soft moans of completion bubbling with the churn of water.

She twisted to kiss him, whispering that he made her feel wild and free.

But Richard knew it was he who'd been released, freed this night from his tortured prison.

The beast in him tamed by the beauty.

Eleven

Richard stirred the eggs in the frying pan, whistling to himself.

"My, what a chipper mood. Wonder what brought that on?"

He smiled, glancing her way, and loving her sexy grin. She'd been teasing him since dawn, and after last night he wondered where she got the energy to wake at this ungodly hour.

"I could take you back upstairs and show you, if you like."

"Upstairs? But there are at least twenty rooms to visit still." Laura snickered to herself, her body jumping to life with the thought of him touching her.

"Twenty is not enough," he said, giving her a meaningful look.

Laura cleared her throat and tried for a little dignity before he had her on the table screaming in ecstasy.

Not that that wasn't a splendid idea. "So other than giving me fantasies, what do you have planned today?" she said.

"Besides watching you?"

"My, how eventful."

He brought the pan to the center island and pushed the eggs into a bowl, then took the pan and utensils to the sink, washed them, dried them and put them away.

Laura blinked, and when he straightened from closing the cabinet, he noticed her expression.

"What?" Briefly, he glanced down at his jeans and bare feet, searching for spilled egg yolk.

"A man who cleans up after himself. Wait till my sisters hear about this."

He made a face. "I've been alone for a long time. If I don't do it, it doesn't get done."

"Keep it up, Blackthorne. I like a man who knows his place is with a dishrag in his hand."

He laughed and caught her as she passed with a plate of bacon. Instantly she set the plate aside as he nuzzled her neck, his arms wrapping her.

"God, you smell good."

"It's the bacon fat. Adds an air of mystery."

He chuckled, turned her in his arms, and kissed her with painfully slow deliberation.

Laura's body heated up much faster and she pushed into him, her hand rubbing over his wide chest clad in a blue cotton T-shirt. When she drew back, she was breathless and dizzy with desire and she brushed his hair off his brow. "I can cut your hair, if you want."

"Don't like the pirate look?" He sent her a lecherous glance, and with the slashing scars, he looked positively dastardly.

"You're too handsome to hide behind all that hair."

He grinned. Somehow when she called him handsome, he wanted to believe her. "Tonight, then." He kissed her lightly, then they parted and went back to making breakfast.

Munching on some bacon, Richard put bread into the toaster as Laura took out plates and silverware, setting places for four. Dewey popped in every morning for coffee, but she wasn't expecting Kelly to be up for another hour.

Richard opened the refrigerator for the butter, and when he closed it, Laura stood rock still at the far end of the wood counter.

He frowned and turned.

Kelly stood near the entrance, her hair sleep-tousled, her teddy bear clutched to her side.

Panic ripped through him. Oh, God. His child. She'd see his scars.

His gaze shot to Laura's, and she recognized his dread. It was one thing for her to see him and accept him. Quite another for a four-year-old.

"Good morning, Kelly," Laura said, and only Richard noticed the break in her voice. She reached for him, keeping him where he stood when he wanted to turn his back to his daughter.

Kelly knuckled her eyes and yawned. "Morning, Miss Laura. Hi, Daddy." She climbed up into her chair, put her bear in the seat beside her, then glanced between the adults. "Are you having breakfast with us, Daddy?"

She looked expectantly at him. Sweetly innocent. Trustingly. Not at all afraid of him.

Richard cleared his throat twice before he managed to say, "Yes, princess, I am."

"Oh, goody." She reached for a slice of bacon, chomping into it as Laura leaned across the counter to pour her some juice.

Laura looked at Richard. He was frozen, gazing down at his baby, and she detected the sheen of tears in his blue eyes. Laura set the pitcher down and crossed to him.

He kept staring at Kelly. "She doesn't even realize." His voice was rough, and after a moment, he dragged his gaze to Laura.

She smiled. "Another female you've underestimated, huh?" She swept the backs of her fingers across his cheek.

"Yes," he choked, grasping her hand. "Yes." Then he smiled and Laura felt her heart lift with the pure joy of it.

He started for Kelly. Laura laid her hand on his arm, stopping him. "Go slow."

He nodded, not wanting to frighten his daughter, and when the toast popped up, he turned quickly to the counter to butter it. "Do you like jelly, Kelly?"

His daughter laughed. "Blueberry is my favorite."

"Yeah, yeah," Laura said, rolling her eyes. "It was grape yesterday. And before that, peach." She tickled the child, giving her a smacky good-morning kiss on the cheek. Richard turned back to the counter and set the plate in front of his daughter. Then he slid into the chair and, with Laura at his side, watched his daughter in the simple morning ritual of having her breakfast.

The day, he thought, could not get any better.

The wind snapped at Laura's coat, and though the rain had stopped for a while, it didn't look like it would hold off for long.

"Come with us," Laura said.

"You two go on and have a girl afternoon."

"Please, Daddy," Kelly said from the passenger seat of the SUV.

Laura put her hand on Kelly's arm, stopping her pleas. She tried to understand Richard's apprehension. For over a week they'd lived without the shadows hiding each other. But for Richard to test the waters with the public was a step he wasn't willing to take. Not yet, anyway. The townsfolk hadn't been very receptive to him from the start, and to them all, he was still the beast in the castle. They whispered about him, made him into the mysterious creature that he once was. Once. Not anymore. But getting the townsfolk to grow accustomed to him would take time.

And getting Richard to take that step forward was even harder.

She felt as if he was dragging his heels.

"It's okay," she said to him. "We won't be long."

"I want to," he said softly. "But not with Kelly near. I don't know what I'd do if she heard some of the things they've called me."

Laura's lips tightened. "Me, neither."

He touched her face, tipping her chin up, and loving how she was so ready to defend Kelly and him, as she had in the past weeks.

"Does this mean you'll be with me and Kelly but not anyone else?"

"I can't. Not right now."

Her temper jumped. "This won't work forever, Richard. There are teacher conferences, Girl Scouts, ballet lessons. Will you deny Kelly and yourself a life because of what people *might* say?"

He arched a brow at the sudden surge of anger.

"No, but you want me to jump in the deep end of the pool first off."

She sighed hard. "Okay, okay. I understand. Or at least I'm trying to. Maybe it's too much, too soon." She glanced at Kelly, who wasn't interested in the adults and played with the buttons and dials on the dashboard. Laura looked back at Richard. "I care about you both," she said softly, and his smile appeared. "I want you to be happy, and hiding with you is not what Kelly needs."

"Or you?"

"Yes."

Richard let out a harsh breath. He knew this was coming. She'd hinted at it enough in the last couple of days. But this was not a discussion to have right now. "We can talk about this tonight, okay?"

"Oh, you bet we will."

He loved the belligerent look she gave him, her determination written from the top of her cute ponytail to her worn sneakers. But he wasn't going to trot down the middle of Main Street and wait for the ridicule. And as for the future, Richard couldn't think that far ahead, yet as he gazed down at her, he knew she'd stolen more than his heart. And he'd given it freely. He wanted these feelings to last forever, to keep the world from intruding, and standing before anyone else except her, Kelly and Dewey would ruin it.

"Tonight, then." He bent to kiss her.

Kelly giggled. Richard winked at her. His daughter had accepted him and his relationship with Laura. They were a family, she was his lover, and every morning when he woke with her in his arms, he experienced all over again a feeling of such peace and utter contentment that he knew he'd never felt this wonderful before. He would do nothing to jeopardize it. Nothing.

"You better get going before the rain breaks again." He kissed his daughter, then walked around the SUV with Laura.

She slid behind the wheel and buckled the seat belt, pausing to check Kelly's belt. He leaned into the car and kissed her again.

"Hurry back, baby," he said against her lips before he straightened.

"We won't be more than an hour." Laura was going to pick up milk and eggs, and maybe something to occupy Kelly during the next bout of rain. The grocery delivery was backlogged for a day, and she needed some time outside. Not that she didn't mind being with Richard and making love with him, sleeping with him.

Each morning she hustled to her room before Kelly woke, and although he'd argued with her about it, she wasn't going to have the child asking questions neither could answer without creating more. Besides, Richard hadn't said that he wanted this relationship to go further than what it was, and questions from Kelly would prompt that. What was she supposed to say? Are you prepared to make an honest woman out of me? Do you expect me to hide with you? Do you really care about me or do you just see a handy lover and a mother for Kelly? Her throat tightened. She was asking for trouble if she kept thinking like this.

Frowning, he stepped back, and she rolled up the window, then started the engine. It stalled once and she blushed and tried again, throwing it into gear and driving down the long path to the gates. It seemed like she was leaving one world and entering another. Gone from the castle house on the hill, into the land of the serfs, she thought with a reluctant smile.

She glanced and saw him in the rearview mirror. He waved and she returned it, then flipped on the radio. She'd learned so much about him in the last days. Aside that he was an incredible lover, an attentive father, and made her indecently happy. He was also a formidable businessman, too. Although she'd known that he'd owned a couple of computer software companies and ran them from the computers in his suite, she hadn't realized he'd created the software himself. Software for small and large businesses—security programs, antivirus programs, games, search sites, graphics. There was nothing he couldn't create, she'd realized after seeing his work. He'd made boatloads of money and never set foot off this land. No wonder he didn't feel the need to hurry into the public eye.

She and Kelly were pulling into the grocery store parking lot when the music on the radio suddenly stopped. She frowned as the DJ came on with a special news report. The tropical storm off the coast of Florida had just been upgraded to a hurricane. A big one. And it was headed this way.

Richard snapped back the curtain and glared at the darkness quickly cloaking the land. The wind howled furiously but produced little rain. But it would come, and he wondered what was keeping Laura. They'd been gone too long.

He'd tried the cell phone number, but it kept saying she was out of the area. It was bunk, unless she hopped on the ferry, but cell phones were a piece of technology he couldn't understand. Turn a corner and it wouldn't work. Go into one building and it would.

Either way, he was impatient to see them, to make certain they were safe. To hold his girls in his arms.

He dialed the police, but the line was busy, and he knew with the hurricane threatening the coast it would be hours before they could go looking for a missing woman and child. Without a second thought, Richard strode to the closet, tossed on a coat and headed outside. He asked Dewey if he could borrow his truck, and when the man tossed him the keys, Dewey offered to go look. Richard waved him off, unable to sit still any longer, and asked the man to start securing the grounds.

Moments later, he was driving down the main road at a dangerous speed, the rain pounding at the roof and windows as he searched. He flipped on the floodlights mounted on the top of the cab, spinning the handle and sending a million watts of light over the darkened streets. This is likely the only time all this good ol' boy hardware came in handy, he thought, and was grateful for it. Rain washed over the street, creating gullies. Mud and sand had already trapped cars, and he imagined the SUV stuck and the water rushing up the door. He swung the light left and right, creeping slowly down street after street and wishing he could go faster.

Then he spotted them. Relief crashed through him as he pulled up alongside and climbed out. Over the engine and the rain he heard the faint sound of singing as he rushed to the side of the SUV.

Laura rolled down the window and blinked at him. "Richard!"

The shock on her face cut him in half. She hadn't expected him to leave the house for her. It shamed him and he leaned close and kissed her hard. "Thank God."

"Hi, Daddy," Kelly called.

"Are you two okay?" He flung open the car door and sent the window up.

"Yes, the engine stalled and wouldn't start," she said, climbing out and reaching over the seat for Kelly. "Then the cell phone battery died while I was trying to call. I forgot to recharge it."

Richard took Kelly from her, then helped them into the warm truck, before he went to the SUV for the packages. "Good Lord, Laura," he muttered, stuffing the bags around their feet. "Think you have enough?"

"I heard about the hurricane. I wanted us to be prepared."

Us, he thought. Was she already thinking of them as a family, like he was? "We're getting some of it," he said. "Maybe it will scoot up the coast like the last one." Hurricanes were bad if you lived on the coast, horrific if you lived on an island like this. It was the price of solitude and beautiful sunsets, he thought dismally.

Securing the SUV and climbing into the truck he took a deep breath, let it out, then looked at Kelly and Laura. He didn't know what he'd do if anything had happened to them. Suddenly Kelly flung herself in his arms.

"I knew you would come for us, Daddy."

He squeezed her, looking over her head at Laura.

Her smile was tender and pleased. "You left the house for us."

Laura was still stunned.

"I couldn't very well let my best girls sit in a storm without me."

She reached over and sifted her fingers through his wet hair. She was proud of him, but she didn't have to say so. He knew. It was another step into the land of the living.

He grasped her hand, bringing it to his lips.

"Is Serabi okay, Daddy?"

Richard let Laura go, then smiled down at his daughter. So like a kid to be oblivious to the danger, he thought. "She was sleeping by the fire when I left," he said, buckling her in, then driving toward home.

"I say it's a hot-chocolate-and-cartoon-movie night," Laura said. "Warm jammies, popcorn, a real slug feast."

Kelly clapped and snuggled between the two adults, smiling brightly despite the rain flooding around them.

The chance to talk never came. The storm grew stronger and there was too much to do to prepare. Wearing jeans and a sweatshirt, Laura helped Richard and Dewey secure the yard and the stables. Dewey had already towed the SUV back to the house and it was tucked in the garage. He'd insisted it was his fault, and he'd work on it during the storm.

Richard fed and curried the horses, then secured them in their stalls. They were fortunate that the house was high on a hill, and if the waters reached them, then the entire village would be lost before then. When Richard told her that she and Kelly would need to pack a few things and be ready to take the next ferry, Laura stalled, finding something else that needed to be locked down. She wasn't leaving this island without him and that was all there was to it.

And he wouldn't go.

So she made preparations to wait out the storm.

She had already placed flashlights and candles within reach all over the house. Though Richard had a generator and it was primed in case the power went out, she wasn't taking any chances. The "Caine" wasn't close yet, but they were feeling some of its power. Kelly had her own personal flashlight and Laura had to keep telling her to turn it off, that the electricity was still working and the battery would go dead when she needed it. Finally she had to put it on top of the fridge.

When they made it back inside, Kelly was watching a video with her kitten, so entranced she didn't even look up. Laura hung their coats in the back mudroom, then prepared a pot of coffee.

"I want you to take the next ferry off the island. Go to a hotel and stay there."

"There won't be any hotel rooms available till Columbia. Everyone on the coast is moving inland." Flipping on the coffeemaker, she faced him. "Are you coming with us?"

"Of course not."

"Forget it then."

"Laura, you need to get inland."

"No, Richard. I'm not leaving you here."

"I'm a big boy."

Her gaze moved over him from head to foot. "I know." Her lips quirked. "But I'm still not going."

"You are, dammit, if I say you are!"

She folded her arms over her middle. "Make me."

"Dammit, Laura, can't you see the danger?"

"Don't you swear at me, Blackthorne. If Kelly and I leave, then you and Dewey have to come, too."

"Like hell." He reached for the phone and dialed.

"If I have to drag you two to the boat and strap you in, you're getting to safety."

"We are safe here. Safer than we'd be driving through the rain trying to find a motel. And probably safer than the rest of the village!"

He spoke to the ferry offices, asking when the next boat left. He barked at the man on the other end of the line, then apologized and hung up.

"Well, you have your way. There are no more ferries leaving."

"It's no wonder, look at the water."

He did, glancing out the windows. Whitecaps foamed, smashing on the shore. No sooner than one crested, then another crashed onto the beach. Wind shrieked though the trees and the clouds blanketed the stars. He looked back at her. "You did that on purpose. Arguing with me, finding one more chore to do till it was too late."

She shrugged, fighting a smile. He scowled blackly.

Laura crossed to him, stopping close and slipping her arms around his trim waist.

"I'm exactly where I want to be, Richard. If we were apart right now all you would do was worry over whether or not Kelly and I had made it to safety. At this point we'd be inching along with a million other people fleeing inland and you know it."

He softened, closing his arms around her.

"Yeah, I guess you're right."

"'Bout killed you to admit that, huh?"

"No."

"Liar, liar, pants on fire." She smiled at his sour look. "Besides, we still have a lot more rooms to christen."

He grinned slowly.

"And I do so love a good storm."

"You're twisted."

"Nah, just need that thunder to drown out my screaming when you do that thing you do with your hips."

"Oh, Laura," he groaned, and kissed her, his hands mapping her body and diving under her sweatshirt. He shaped her ribs, her breast, all the while kissing her and wanting her naked and ready for him.

She made a little sound in the back of her throat, pulling him harder against her.

"Is it bedtime yet?" he whispered, worrying her lips.

"In a little while."

"Damn."

She laughed softly, and when Kelly called to them, they parted.

Richard stepped back, gripping the counter and motioning to her. "You'd better go see what's up."

"I can see what's *up*," she said, laughing harder as she went to his daughter.

Richard just grinned and wondered how he'd managed to live without her in his life.

In the grand bed in the tower Richard pushed into her body, each stroke bringing them closer and closer to rapture. He watched her face, the sight more erotic than their joining as he retreated and slid smoothly home.

She gasped each time he did.

Outside the storm raged. Inside passion ruled.

She dug her heels into the mattress, rising up to greet him, their cadence smooth and quickening. He leaned down, his forehead pressed to hers as he thrust harder and watched ecstasy spread over her features as it peeled through her body.

And pulled him into his climax.

He ground to her, her womanly muscles clasping him, wringing him, and he never felt more vulnerable than in this moment. Nor more powerful.

Laura let the sinful pleasure swamp her, bathe her as he shuddered hard, spilling into her with a low growl. She felt shattered, her quivering body buffeting with delicious sensations and drumming them down to her soul.

"Oh, Richard, Richard," she gasped, pulling him down onto her, wrapping her limbs around him.

She kissed his throat, his scarred cheek, as the passion slowly faded and they sank back to earth. Neither spoke, neither knowing what to say or if they should put words to thoughts.

But Laura silently admitted them. She'd fallen deeply, madly in love with him. Her tender beast, her scarred prince. And she was afraid that she'd get what she deserved. Another broken heart.

And this one, she knew, would never heal.

Twelve

The hurricane was named Helen, and she was vengeful and mean when she was riled.

Typhoons of water coiled in the center of the river side of Moss Island. Even the marsh side waved like molasses, thick mud rising up and lowering with the power of the wind. On the sea side of the plot of paradise, waves curled twenty feet high, slapping down on the seawall like a pale white hand punishing the islanders who dared lived so close to the ocean.

Laura loved it. She wouldn't have, though, if she hadn't known she was safe in the large stone manor.

The rain sounded like tacks on a wood floor, the thunder like the crack of breaking wood. So far. She knew it would get worse and kept her ear tuned to the radio reports. The nearly airtight doors and windows occasionally pulsed with the change of the wind. All the glass was boarded over or taped. Outside, sandbags lined the living room French doors, and inside she'd laid towels and rags to absorb the water the wind forced under the door frame. It was the only spot in the house that was their concern.

Kelly watched TV or played with her dolls while Richard moved from room to room checking seals, then climbing into the uppermost rooms and the attic, assuring himself that the roof wasn't leaking.

She entered the yellow room, not flipping on the lights, and because the power had already flickered several times today, she used the battery-operated lantern. She went to the window and gazed down at the empty town. The last ferry had taken nearly everyone except the police off the island yesterday.

A sharp, loud crack of lightning split the black sky for several seconds, lighting the land below the house. My God, she thought.

"Richard," she called. "Come quick."

He rushed into the room. "You shouldn't be near that window," he said, coming to her side. "It's not taped."

She was still staring down at the village. "The wind hits from the sea side, not here," she said, then looked back over her shoulder. "But there are people still down there."

"What!" He rushed to the window.

"The town is flooding. When the lightning flashed, I saw the police four-by-four. The cop looked like he was trying to get them to safety." She pointed, yet knew he couldn't see anything in the dark. "We have to do something."

"I thought they were all on the mainland."

During every hurricane for the past five years, the island had been completely evacuated, except for the police. And him. Richard couldn't stand by and watch them suffer when he was on safe ground. From his pocket, he pulled the two-way radio he'd been using to keep in contact with Dewey and told him the situation.

"Get your truck. Does that police radio you keep still work?"

"Yeah, and I've been listening to the scanner. Old Mrs. Demmer's place is under two feet of water and it's creeping up Magnolia Street." Dewey's voice scraped over the radio.

"Then we have to move fast. Radio the deputy."

"I hear you. I'll get them up here."

Richard pocketed the small radio and motioned to Laura. "Come on. We need to find blankets and pillows." He turned out of the room and headed downstairs. "Medical supplies. Make some coffee, I guess." He paused on the staircase, looking back at her. "Do we have enough food to last a couple days?"

"Yes, and I can make it stretch."

"Good. I have no idea how many are stranded down there." He continued down the stairs. "I feel like an idiot for not thinking of it."

"You didn't have any reason to. We thought everyone was gone but us."

"This is going to be a hairy couple of nights."

"Heck, darlin', you haven't seen hairy till you've tried to keep a goat happy in your kitchen and from eating your momma's good tablecloths." She darted past him, heading to the kitchen.

He laughed softly. "Goats, Laura?" He tsked softly. "What would the pageant people think of that?"

"They'd probably take my crowns." She paused

and turned back, cupping his cheek and kissing his chiseled mouth. "Now ask me if I care?"

He smiled, patted her behind, and she gave him a saucy look before rushing into the kitchen and flipping on the lights. "Blankets and pillows are in the upstairs first closet. Take the ones out of my bedroom, too. I saw four in the closet in there." She'd rearranged everything, so he'd be hunting all night for them. "I think there are two afghans in the chest in the library, and I bet if we look hard," she said, "we can hustle up a half dozen more."

As she spoke, she put on a fresh pot of coffee, got out some thermoses and started making sandwiches.

Richard went to look for candles and lanterns as well. He didn't have the heart to tell her that when it came to being with these people, she was on her own.

Laura poured coffee, glancing at Lisa Tolar, a lovely young woman who'd come here with her new husband for their honeymoon. Rotten timing, she thought. At least they'll have something interesting to tell their children. Lisa pitched in quickly, and her husband, a marine from Beaufort, was just as helpful, pouring coffee and drinks, working the VCR and keeping everyone calm. A trivia game helped pass the time and ease the unfamiliarity between the stranded. On the floor with Kelly was only one other child. Christopher Austin, a darling little redheaded boy with *Irish* written in his pale eyes and freckles. His parents sat a few feet away as the children colored. There were three others, including the two police officers, Andrew and Mark, and they went out together to check on things periodically. But there was nothing to check on.

The island was empty except for all the people in the Blackthorne house.

And everyone was in the living room, dining room and kitchen.

Except for Richard.

This was his chance, she thought. He'd opened his home to them, surely they wouldn't ridicule him? Not in front of Kelly. No one could be that heartless.

It was ticking her off the longer he stayed away. And that he hadn't told her he was going to remain hidden.

"Where is Mr. Blackthorne?" the police officer, Mark Lindsey, asked.

Laura shrugged. "Somewhere in the house, I suspect."

"Have you seen him?"

"Of course."

"What's he look like?"

Kelly looked up, glancing between the young policeman and Laura.

"Handsome, tall." Laura crossed to Mark and filled his cup. "Try not to be so crass, Officer Lindsey. He's just a man. A man, I might add, who has opened his home to you and everyone else here."

He blushed and sipped his coffee.

Just then Kelly put down her crayons and stood, walking into the wide hall, then to the staircase.

Laura heard her voice, then Richard's deep murmur. Kelly came rushing back in and stopped short.

"Here he is." She looked back over her shoulder and motioned.

Richard did not appear.

Kelly marched back into the shadows, and a few moments later, she came forward, her hand clasped in

Richard's as she led him into the light. "This is my daddy."

Richard gazed down at his little girl, so touched by her gesture, the back of his throat burned. With a deep breath, he stepped forward and tipped his head back, giving them a look at the beast.

Laura set the carafe down and moved to him, standing by his side, slipping her hand in his and waiting for the slings and arrows. The looks of repugnance.

They never came.

"Hello, Mr. Blackthorne," Mark said, walking slowly up to him. "It's a pleasure to finally meet you." They shook hands as Mark introduced himself, his partner, then the others. Richard smiled and nodded, all the while wondering when it would start. When the pain would begin. But nothing happened. Nothing.

When Mark came to the newlyweds, he stumbled over their names.

"Gary and Lisa Tolar," the young woman said. "We're on our honeymoon."

"Hell of a reception you got, huh?" Richard said, and the couple smiled.

Abruptly, glass shattered, spraying the floor behind them all. Richard rushed around the people and furniture, pulling the drapes over the break in the French door. "Mark, in the mudroom is a hammer, nails and some wood planks."

The police officer ran to get them, and he and Richard secured the window, then decided it was best to cover the entire set of doors.

Laura swept the glass as the policemen moved the furniture back from the windows. Richard strode near and knelt with the dustpan. When he straightened, she took the dustpan, and without a word or a glance, went to the kitchen to empty it.

He frowned at her back. Something was wrong, and a niggling of apprehension slithered through him. But he didn't have the chance to talk to her, to get her alone for a moment. There were too many people around. And Richard admitted that he was having a hard time getting used to being near them and slipped into his library. Mark was lounging on the sofa, reading.

The young policeman stood, flushing. "I'm sorry to go nosing around. But this library is incredible." He waved to the shelves of books.

"Borrow whatever you like, Mark. What good are all these books if no one enjoys them?" He crossed to a small lowboy and lifted a decanter.

"This is a first edition."

Richard glanced at the title and the old leather-bound book. "I imagine the author would be quite pleased someone is still reading his work. Feel free."

Richard splashed a bit of brandy into a glass, offering some to the young man. Mark shook his head, claiming to still be on duty.

Richard slipped behind the desk and into the leather chair. For a moment he remembered seeing Laura here, sifting through the papers of his past, the photos, and wearing very little. He wished this storm was over and he could take her to his bed.

He shifted in the chair.

"People were scared of you."

"I know."

"No reason to be, though."

Richard arched a brow.

Mark suddenly loosened his tie and unbuttoned his

shirt, spreading it to show burn scars that covered his chest and shoulder and that were barely visible at the collar of his shirt. "I know how you feel."

Richard slowly lowered the glass.

"I was curious over which of us was worse," Mark said.

"Think it's about equal." Richard gestured to the chair near the desk, kicking it out. "If I may ask, how did it happen?"

The young policeman settled into the chair, buttoning his shirt back up, as he said, "I was married at the time, not out of the police academy two years. I was serving in Orangeburg when we got the call of a fire in the boys' town. It's an orphanage for troubled kids. Anyway, I was the first on the scene...."

For two more days, Hurricane Helen threw a tantrum, then moved north, leaving behind bright sunlight and enough damage to keep everyone busy for a while. On the cool morning, the guests departed and Laura knew she'd made some new friends, while Richard had formed some sort of kinship with the young police officer, Mark. It pleased her. When she woke the following morning and found Richard making Kelly breakfast, Laura experienced a hard pang of regret. He didn't need her anymore. Nor did Kelly. Heck, the child was dressed in appropriate clothes, her long dark hair brushed and clipped in barrettes.

"Good morning," Richard said, and his expression fell at the look in her eyes.

Laura forced a bright smile. "Good morning, you two."

Kelly twisted in her chair, a piece of bacon hanging

out of her mouth. Laura snatched it off, ate it, then kissed the child good morning.

"Did you sleep okay?" Richard asked as she poured herself a cup of coffee. She'd nodded off the instant they'd slipped into bed, and in the morning, as she had done since they they'd started sharing a bed, she'd gone to her room. He wanted to wake with her in his arms.

"Yes, fine. I didn't realize I was so tired."

"You were incredible with all those people," he said

She looked at him over the rim of her cup. "So were you."

Was that sadness he saw in her eyes, he wondered, placing a plate of toast before Kelly.

Laura forced herself to sit through breakfast, although her bags were packed. She didn't want to go, she didn't want to say goodbye. But Richard was capable now and her job was done. Katherine Davenport had already called yesterday with a new assignment.

It was time to go.

God, she felt horrible.

"Kelly and I are going to the grocery this morning, you coming with us?"

"No, I've got some laundry to finish and I'm still a little tired."

Richard came to her, slipping his arms around her. "I missed you last night," he said.

She merely nodded and he tried not to frown at the desolate look in her eyes. "What's wrong?"

"Nothing sleep won't cure."

"Why don't you go back to bed, it's only eight."

"I might," she said, and couldn't bring herself to speak what she was thinking.

A few minutes later Richard and Kelly were tooling down the drive, ready to greet the rest of the island and dispel the gossips once and for all.

Laura cleaned the breakfast dishes, prepared something for dinner and called a cab.

Laura stood on the dock, her eyes burning to hold back tears. She felt severed in half, and she hated leaving the two most important people in her life, but she had no choice. Part of her shouted to stay and be with them as they had been, any way she could. And her heart said he had never asked, never spoken about a future, and maybe she was just reading too much into their relationship. She'd done that with Paul and look what that had gotten her.

Richard knew this was temporary. Her job was done.

"Where the hell do you think you are going?" a voice said from behind.

She stiffened and didn't turn. "Home."

"I thought you *were* home."

The anger in his voice was clear as the sky.

"No, Richard. I came to help you with Kelly, to integrate her into your life so you could be her father."

"And that's it? You're leaving me?"

Her heart shattered at the sorrowful sound of his voice. "I have to," she said.

He grabbed her arm, forcing her around. "Why?"

"I'm finished. My job is done."

His anger flared hard. "What were Kelly and me, a damn charity case?"

"No!"

"So you float into our lives and then skip out? Is that how little you thought of me? Some poor wretched soul you needed to bestow your tenderness on?'' He leaned and lowered his voice. ''Was that what you felt when you let me touch you, taste you?''

''Of course not.'' A single tear escaped, and she let it fall.

''Then why are you doing this?''

''Because I will never know if it's gratitude you feel or more!'' she said in a soft howl.

''Good grief, give me some credit for knowing how I feel.'' He released her and took a step back. ''I'm a grown man and I know what I want, and I want you.''

She shook her head and lifted her gaze. His heart cracked at the tears in her eyes.

''How am I to know if it's still not just transferred emotions? You were alone and hiding. Now you're free and have your daughter and can be her father. How can I be sure?''

''Because I don't need to lean on you anymore. I don't need your help. And I still feel the same.''

She blinked.

Suddenly he was inches from her, crowding her. ''How could you not know? I don't need a crutch, Laura, but I need you in my heart.'' He rubbed her arms, gazing deeply into her green eyes. ''I always will. I can't breathe with the thought of you gone. I can't live without you. Stay, Laura.''

She sobbed without sound, tears streaming down her cheeks.

''I love you,'' he said cupping her face in his broad hands, and she choked on her tears. *''I love you!''* he said fiercely. ''From the moment I saw you. I loved you when you yelled at me for hiding, when you held my daughter and soothed her heartache and kept loving her when I couldn't. I loved you when you fought with me and cursed me." His eyes burned. "I was in a prison, Laura, but loving *you* is my real freedom. Don't send me back there."

She whispered his name, her gaze searching his and seeing her future unfold. "I love you," she said.

"Thank God." He closed his eyes and exhaled, and when he looked at her again, he said, "Marry me, be my wife, my best friend. Take my name, make babies with me, and make me the happiest man alive. I need you, my beauty."

She gazed into his bright blue eyes.

"Say yes," he said, worrying her lips.

"Are you demanding again or asking?"

"Begging."

"Aah, dishrags and begging, my kind of man."

He chuckled, the sound full of old pain and heartache releasing into the cool Carolina air.

"I love you, Richard Blackthorne," she whispered against his lips, then sank into one of his slow, wet kisses that made her toes curl.

"Did she say yes, Daddy? Did she?"

Laura drew back and watched Kelly run from the SUV toward them, all gangly legs and dark hair flying. Richard scooped his daughter up in his arms, and the two of them stared at Laura.

"Are you gonna be my momma now?"

Laura eyed Richard, brushing at her cheek. "Yes, precious, I guess I am."

Kelly smiled beautifully. "See, Daddy, you didn't have to go to the ends of the earth to find her."

Laura smiled, tears of joy forming again as Richard wrapped his arm around her and pressed his forehead to hers. "No, honey. But I would have. I surely would have."

Epilogue

One year later

Laura was just closing up the Blackthorne Gallery when Richard called out to her. She smiled as he climbed out of the SUV and came to her. She worked the key out of the lock, then lifted her gaze to his.

"Hey, darling. You look tired." He kissed her softly.

"Aah, honey." She gripped his arms. "It's time."

"Time for what?"

She gave him a "you are such a man" look and, with both hands, pointed to her large round tummy.

He blinked, his eyes wide. "Right now?"

"Well, the way I've been having contractions all day, I'd say we have about thirty minutes."

Panic swept him. "Good grief, Laura, why didn't you call me?"

"And do what? Sit at home with you staring at me? With my mother and sister hovering over me?"

Okay, he thought, all those women around were hard enough to take. "Can you walk?"

"Sure. And I can dance, too, see?" She did a cute little cha-cha that looked more like a waddle.

"God, don't do that!" He held her still.

She laughed at his panic. "Come on. Let's go get Kelly."

"No, no, the doctor's first. Dewey can get Kelly from school."

"But we promised her."

"She'll just have to understand. Come on." He took her arm. She dug her feet in and he groaned. "Tell me you aren't going to argue with me over this, are you? Now?"

"We promised."

"Good Lord, Laura, you're having my baby. Our baby. We need to get going."

"Got a problem, there, Mr. Blackthorne?" a shop-keeper said, laughing.

Richard looked at him. "She's in labor and won't go to the doctor!" He pointed at her accusingly. "Your sisters are going to have me for breakfast over this."

"I'll go. It's not that big of a rush." A second later she folded over with a contraction. "Oh, mercy, maybe it is. Jeepers, your son is as pushy as you are."

Richard wasn't taking any answer but his own and instantly he lifted her in his arms and put her in the car. Across the street Officer Lindsey hopped on his motorcycle and rode over. "How about a police escort, Richard?"

Richard slid behind the wheel, his hands shaking. "Thanks Mark."

"Oh, don't be ridiculous!" Laura said, and didn't know whether to be embarrassed or amused as Mark turned on his lights and siren and escorted them the whole two blocks to the doctor. Their friends lined the street, waving and shouting good wishes.

Less than an hour later in the small hospital, Richard held his son in his arms. Laura practically delivered on the doorstep and now she was sitting in the bed, Kelly tucked to her side. He laid the baby in her arms, then climbed in with them, pressing his lips to her temple. Kelly counted her little brother's fingers as he tipped Laura's face to his.

"I love you," he whispered, then kissed her deeply, slowly. "Thank you." He slipped a ring on her right hand, a row of their son's birthstone, another right alongside it with blue gems.

"What's the second one for?" she asked.

"It's Kelly's."

Tears blossomed in her eyes, and she kissed him, whispering her love and knowing she couldn't be happier. Her dreams had come true and the proof lay all around her.

Richard snuggled his family in his arms, his life a far cry from those dark nights pacing the hallways, alone. He'd been a bitter, desolate man locked in a dreary tower, and Laura had walked through his doors, stirring his soul and forcing him to come live in her world and see all the gifts it offered. Looking down at his family, he knew how abundant love could be, and he cherished the day she'd stepped into his cage and awakened him. In loving her, he was free, the beast rescued by the beauty and rewarded with her heart.

* * * * *

January 2001
TALL, DARK & WESTERN
#1339 by Anne Marie Winston

February 2001
THE WAY TO A RANCHER'S HEART
#1345 by Peggy Moreland

March 2001
MILLIONAIRE HUSBAND
#1352 by Leanne Banks
Million-Dollar Men

April 2001
GABRIEL'S GIFT
#1357 by Cait London
Freedom Valley

May 2001
**THE TEMPTATION OF
RORY MONAHAN**
#1363 by Elizabeth Bevarly

June 2001
A LADY FOR LINCOLN CADE
#1369 by BJ James
Men of Belle Terre

MAN OF THE MONTH

For twenty years Silhouette has been giving
you the ultimate in romantic reads. Come join
the celebration as some of your favorite authors
help celebrate our anniversary with the most
sensual, emotional love stories ever!

Available at your favorite retail outlet.

Where love comes alive™

LONG, TALL TEXANS

EMMETT, REGAN & BURKE

New York Times
extended list bestselling author

Diana PALMER

**returns to Jacobsville, Texas, in this special
collection featuring rugged heroes, spirited
heroines and passionate love stories told
in her own inimitable way!**

Coming in May 2001 only from Silhouette Books!

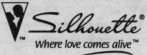
Silhouette®
Where love comes alive™

Visit Silhouette at www.eHarlequin.com   PSLLT

Look in the back pages of
all June Silhouette series books to find an
exciting new contest with fabulous prizes!
Available exclusively through Silhouette.

Don't miss it!

Where love comes alive™

P.S. Watch for details on how you can meet
your favorite Silhouette author.